SEEING BEYOND THE
Shattered Glass

THE STRUGGLE HAS NO HOLD ON THE OUTCOME

Thank you!
Ketra Y. Davenport-Riey
2022

SEEING BEYOND THE

Shattered Glass

THE STRUGGLE HAS NO HOLD ON THE OUTCOME

DR. KETRA L. DAVENPORT-KING

BASED ON TRUE EVENTS

Dedications

To Keenan and Kennedi, thank you for your unconditional love. I am proud to be your mother. To my husband, who loves me just as Christ loves the church – you have been my greatest supporter, and you always allow me the space to spread my wings as I continue my journey to becoming the woman God has called me to *be*.

Special Thanks

To my mother, you are my anchor and strength, your love and support throughout every part of my life molded me into the woman I am today. To my sister, thank you for being my sounding board for everything! Special thanks to my mentors, professors, beta readers, and friends who pushed me to see beyond the shattered glass in my life. Your encouragement from the early morning and late-night calls that allowed me to cry, laugh, and share my thoughts is appreciated. To Pastor Phyllis Johnson, THANK YOU for your consistency and loyalty; your words of wisdom will forever be an imprint on my heart.

Credits

Latrise Sheriff and Stephanie Wynn, Cover Design
Tavia, cover photo – *For Beauty Sake*
Tavia, MUA – *For Beauty Sake*
Brian Smith, Editor

"Seeing Beyond the Shattered Glass is riveting! A transparent story of Kassidie that is, unfortunately, a story of so many young girls who remain silent. I asked myself as I read this book, how does anyone retain a semblance of sanity, let alone become a beacon of light and hope for others who have experienced something so damaging. She was Shattered! Yet, by the grace of God, somehow, she has been able to put her life back together again.

Ketra is a mother, daughter, sister, and my lovely wife. Since the moment we met, I knew she was no ordinary lady, living an ordinary life. She is empathic, unique, intelligent, and beautiful, all of the dynamic qualities, I believe, were shaped in the crucible fire of sexual abuse and the struggles that she overcame! She is a precious gift from God, and as you read this story, you will laugh, cry, and rejoice through her life's journey toward VICTORY."

~ Pastor Willie L. King, Husband

About the Author

Dr. Ketra L. Davenport-King has served in ministry for over 20 years. As a speaker, advocate, business consultant, mentor, and educator, she has inspired women, men, boys, and girls to speak their truth and take back their lost voice. In 2004, she opened the doors to Life After Advocacy Group, Inc., a non-profit organization that helps women, children, and men reclaim their lives from all origins of sexual assault. She is a testimony of God's ability to turn your most significant pain into your greatest blessing. Ketra currently resides in Dallas, TX, with her husband and is the proud mother of two adult children and her dog, Kobe.

Foreword

There are few things in life more important than being a father. I happen to believe that most, if not all, personal "baggage" people carry around with them can be traced back to something their father did or did not do—daddy issues. The woman who believes that if a man isn't physically or emotionally abusive toward her, then he doesn't love her probably didn't have a father around who showed her what love from a man is supposed to look like. The man who doesn't provide emotional and financial support to his children most likely didn't have a father around to instill the importance of being a provider. Children who are disrespectful to authority figures often display that behavior because they didn't have a father figure around to enforce rules and instill discipline. I could go on for days giving examples of the ramifications of not having an influential father figure in one's life, but you see my point.

When Ketra approached me about helping her with this book, I was taken aback when I heard what she'd gone through with her father. It was another example of how a father's failure to protect can have a lifelong impact on his kids. My emotions swayed from shock to anger, but once I gathered my bearings and realized this was a story of triumph, helping her put it into book form and disseminated to the world became my sole focus.

Ketra has more than survived—she has excelled. More importantly, her success is a testament to God's ability to turn tragedy into triumph if we allow the *word* to be our source of strength.

I entered into this partnership, having more experience in the literary industry than Ketra but quickly recognized that she is much farther along in her spiritual walk than I am. After being exposed to her viewpoint on *forgiveness*, I examined my inability to forgive those whom I feel have wronged me. I now realize that God sent me a spiritual mentor disguised as someone in need of literary mentorship. Won't He do it!

~ Brian W. Smith
Bestselling Author

Prologue

"Kassidie, come here."

While I sat on the floor with my legs crossed, elbows planted on my knees, and my face resting in the palms of my hands, I could hear my father, Kellen's, deep voice barreling down the hallway, but my six-year-old eyes were glued to the television screen. J.J., the star of my favorite show, *Good Times*, clapped his hands, wiggled his lanky body, and shouted, "Dy-no-mite!" I said the phrase right along with him and smiled. When his sister, Thelma, entered the frame, my smile widened. Nothing in the world was more important to me at that moment than watching the two of them rhythmically exchange insults until their father demanded they stop.

I was still giggling at J.J.'s goofiness when my own father's assertive tone—much like the tone often used by J.J.'s television dad, James—plowed through the cacophony created by the show's laugh track.

"Kassidie, come here. I have something to show you."

The command pinched my ear like an angry parent trying to discipline a wayward child in a public place. My head snapped around, and I saw my father—all six-three, two hundred thirty pounds of him—the Incredible Hulk in blackface. With two long strides, he moved within ten feet of me and extended one of his frying pan size hands. I watched his thick fingers wiggle, beckoning me to come over. When the wind blows, leaves have no choice but to submit freely—so I did.

At six years old, I'd never heard the phrase *fight or flight*. Now, I understand that the churning in my stomach and the way my legs felt like limp spaghetti as my father led me to the bedroom, was my body's nervous system going into alarm mode. But when you are a child and your biggest protector is leading you into a dark bedroom, the desire to fight or flee diminishes. After all, who better to put your trust in than the man you witnessed crush a beer can in his bare hand. Any creature lurking under the bed would surely scurry like a roach.

Unfortunately, I was too young to recognize that the most threatening creature in our house that day was the one holding my tiny hand.

Maybe daddy has a surprise for me, I reasoned.

I craned my neck in time to see him look down at me. The affection that usually embodied his stare was absent. His gaze that day was so salacious it groped me.

"Sit down, Kassidie."

My hand trembled when he released it. There was something weird about the way he acted, a weirdness that made the hairs on my forearm stand at attention.

"What's wrong, daddy?"

"Nothing. I want you to sit on the bed."

My parents' bed seemed to be as large as a trampoline. I often bounced and flipped on it with no fear of falling off. But as I surveyed the flower-print comforter, I could sense that my experience on their bed this time would be far from fun.

What happened next changed me. In fact, all that I am today and all that I've been through—the good, bad, and ugly—can be traced back to what happened once I sat on my parents' bed that day.

"Now, move up by the pillows and lay down."

"Are we taking a nap, daddy?"

He didn't reply. Instead, he moved to the side of the bed and sat down. Without saying a word, he pulled off my pants and pulled down my panties.

What are you doing, daddy? That question wanted to spring from my mouth, but fear kept it trapped behind my pressed lips.

Through tear-filled eyes, I watched my father unbuckle his belt. The jeans dropped, and the huge buckle clanked when it hit the floor. I clutched my bottom lip between my teeth and struggled to stifle a scream when he pulled down his underwear.

Why are you doing this, daddy? That was the new question dancing on my tongue. It, too, was imprisoned, lobbying to get out.

He got in the bed. I flinched at the touch of his sweaty palm. Stinging tears streamed down my face and left tracks that I can sometimes see to this day.

Please stop. That was the last thing I remember thinking before my eyes closed, and his tongue slithered along my chest, down my curve-less body, and nestled between my legs.

The buzzer on the coffee table was as attention-grabbing as the zap of a taser. My eyes darted around the room. Sweat beads dotted my forehead. I rose from my prone position on the couch and stared aimlessly at the window.

"It's okay, Kassidie." Dr. Riggio, the woman who managed to unearth my darkest secret, leaned forward in her chair and placed a comforting hand on my knee. "Breathe Kassidie."

"I'm sorry," I mumbled and used the heel of my hand to wipe away tears. "I just...I..."

"We had a breakthrough. That's a good thing."

I swung my legs around and sat on the edge of the couch. Slower breaths replaced the short choppy ones, but the anxiety that left me wide-eyed and panting moved down to my leg. I fidgeted like a teenage girl waiting to hear the results of a pregnancy test.

"That's the first time I've ever told anyone that story."

"I know it is. When pain has been locked away for as long as you've kept yours, getting to it can take some time. It took some time, but you finally released it."

I nodded in agreement.

"Next week, we can talk more about how that pain has impacted you and the decisions you've made throughout your life. Kassidie, this is a good thing."

"I hear you," I said and stood up, "but if it's such a good thing, why do I feel so sick?"

Dr. Riggio leaned back in her chair, draped one leg over the other, and pointed at the bathroom door in the corner of her massive office.

I followed the direction of her manicured finger and made a beeline to the bathroom. The next five minutes consisted of me puking up everything inside of me—including those innocent questions that had been trapped in my mouth since the day my father molested me.

Speaking Out

"We delight in the beauty of the butterfly, but rarely admit the changes it has gone through to achieve that beauty."

~ Maya Angelou

Chapter 1

The treks from Dr. Riggio's office to my car took forever. My steps were measured as if the slightest crack in the aging sidewalk could make me stumble. Puddles gathered in my eyes, but the thought of having bystanders stare at me was enough to keep the tears trapped. However, when I sat down in my car, all that changed. My forehead kissed the steering wheel. My eyelids slammed shut. Nickel-sized tears spilled. Groans sequestered for decades, rumbled in my belly, and raced through my parted lips. The purge had officially begun.

I pulled into my driveway and walked inside of a house that hasn't known laughter in a while. My husband, Carl, is an IT Consultant. His primary client is Uncle Sam. Wherever there is a need for his expertise in Information Security on classified projects, that's where he's going. China last year and Europe the year before that. Now he's on a four-month assignment to Seoul, Korea. Since we are empty nesters (my son is 23 years old and on his own; my daughter is an 18-year-old college freshman who couldn't wait to live on campus), he asked if I wanted to accompany him. I don't speak the language, and I'm not a big fan of kimchi, so I respectfully declined.

Another reason why I declined my husband's offer is that I don't have time to travel abroad. I run a non-profit organization that specializes in helping the victims of sexual abuse and molestation. My staff is small; therefore, my presence is always needed. Let's just say I'm the chief cook and bottle washer. Being away from the office for more than three days is a pipe dream.

I've given you two reasons why I didn't accompany my husband on his trip to Korea, but they aren't the main reasons. The main reason I didn't go is I needed to seek counseling, and I wanted to go to counseling without Carl knowing about it. He flew out of Dallas/Ft Worth International Airport on a Saturday morning. I doubt that he had unpacked his bags and was settled in the country good by the time I had my first session with Dr. Riggio on that following Thursday.

Exhausted to the point of nearly falling asleep with my clothes on, I made my way to the bathroom, determined to wash away the stress that clung to my body. I sat in bathwater hot enough to melt skin and scrubbed. In fact, I rubbed my skin so hard that welts formed on my arm. The skin on the tips of my fingers wrinkled. Sweat lathered my forehead and scalp. Unfortunately, scrubbing the dirt off your skin does not wash away the dirt from your past.

I rested the back of my head on the tub and closed my eyes. My mind raced. Images from my past fluttered in my mind like an old movie reel. If I had to caption the picture that choked my thoughts at that moment, I'd call it *Inadequate*.

From the day my father stole my innocence, I felt inadequate. I was already a shy child who struggled with establishing friendships, but after he led me into that bedroom, my social anxiety hung around my neck like one of those clunky gold chains rappers wore in the 1980s. My thick lips, lack of curves, and gangly frame made me feel like the butt of every joke—even when the people around me were ignoring me.

By my teenage years, trying to make friends was nearly impossible for me. To compensate for my feelings of inadequacy, I resorted to bribery. I offered classmates money, clothes, food, and anything else I thought might make me more likable. It didn't work. Girls would hang out with me until they'd milked me for whatever they wanted and then toss me aside like an old wash towel. As soon as I healed from the exploitation of one fake friend, another girl would come along and wipe the dust off me, only to use me up and toss me aside again. Ten-dollar whores got better treatment than I did.

The desire to end it all was at its highest by the time I reached my senior year in high school. Contemplating ways to leave this earth became my norm until I was distracted. The distraction came in the form of a handsome boy named Byron. He was a star on the football team. We had several classes together. I often sat in the back of the class and watched as girls lobbied for his attention, and boys struggled to be in his presence as if proximity would earn them a tiny piece of the attention he often ignored.

One day, the boy who everyone knew spoke to the girl that everyone ignored.

The class was like a hip-hop concert. The teacher was late, and the students were shouting, tossing paper balls, writing inappropriate, ill-advised messages on the chalkboard, and a bunch of other crazy things that would be deemed detention worthy.

"Did you do the homework that we have to turn in today?"

I had my head buried in a Harlequin novel that I'd found at home, so I didn't see the face of the person asking the question. I peered over the top edge of the book and saw his belt buckle. My eyes scanned slowly upward: past his mid-section, chest, broad shoulders, and then on his face. It was Byron Carter. *The* Byron Carter. Suddenly, the desire to urinate made me cross my legs.

Byron smiled and flashed dimples that were deep enough for me to stash my book, gather up my things, curl up my long legs, and climb inside.

"Hello," he waved his hand in front of my face, "Is anyone home?"

"Oh, hey," I said. "My mind drifted. What did you say?"

"I asked if you did the homework. Ms. Charles gon' be comin' in here any second, and I don't have it. By the way, my name is—"

"Byron! You're Byron Carter."

"Oh, you know me. What's your name?"

"Kassidie...Kassidie Noel Winters."

He laughed. "Ooookay. Hey, Kassidie."

Oh my God, did I just give him my full name? I know I must sound like a retard. How could you be so stupid, Kassidie? Why don't you give him your address and social security number too?

"Umm, yeah. I got it right here."

"Can I copy it?"

His question was devoid of any shame. When you are seventeen years old and accustomed to groupies bending over backward for you, coaches turning a blind eye to your transgressions and teachers grading on a curve to ensure you are eligible to play. Why wouldn't you expect the nerdy girl in class to offer up the homework she took the time to complete.

"Sure."

Byron plopped down in the chair next to mine and asked, "You got some paper and a pencil I can use?"

This dude didn't even bring his own pencil and paper to cheat.

"Yeah, I got some right here."

He copied my work with an intensity often reserved for the SAT exam. While he scribbled, I stared at him like he was a professional athlete signing an autograph. After a few seconds of gawking, I managed to pry my eyes from him and was stunned to find that all the chaos around me had stopped. Everyone in the class was staring back at me, …sitting next to Byron. Their heads tilted the way a dog tilts its head when trying to figure out what a human is doing.

What the hell are y'all looking at? I thought. *Trust me. This was only a thought. I was never bold enough to speak my mind that way.*

I slowly raised my Harlequin book to cover my face and slumped in my seat.

"There. Finished." Byron said and smiled.

Before I could comment, Ms. Charles entered the room wearing her trademark scowl, a flower print dress that tickled her ankles, and cheap perfume that managed to swallow the stench created by teenage boys who forgot to put on deodorant.

"Thanks, Kassidie Noel Winters," Byron said and winked.

Byron moved back toward the front of the class, where he usually sat. The other kids sat down. Ms. Charles started lecturing, but to me, her words were garbled—like the adult characters in the old *Peanuts* cartoon.

I planted my elbows on the desktop and rested my chin in the palms of my hands. I have no way of knowing, but I'm sure little hearts were in my eyes while I stared at the back of Byron's perfectly shaped head.

He remembered my name.

When I allowed Byron to copy my homework that day, I had no idea it would impact my social standing. He started acknowledging me in the hallways. Once our classmates saw him talking to me, they started talking to me. Girls who often brushed past me as if I was a piece of old furniture, started flashing smiles and speaking as if they'd never treated me like an inanimate object. Popular boys started to flirt with *me*—the girl with shoulders like a wire hanger and legs too long to hide.

One day, I made a pit stop in the restroom and stayed a little too long. By the time I exited the stall, the bell had rung, and the hallways were empty. My class was on the second floor, so I ran toward the nearest stairwell. When I turned the corner, I ran into Byron. I bounced off his broad chest and staggered back like an opposing teams' quarterback. I dropped the two books I held.

"Whoa!" he said. "Girl, you gon' kill somebody."

"I…I'm sorry. I'm late for my third period."

He picked up my books. I reached for them, but he lifted them above his head.

"How bad do you want them?"

"Byron, I'm already late."

He shook his head and flashed those dimples again. I froze. I don't know what I mumbled, but whatever I said made him laugh. And then, it happened. Byron placed his fingers under my chin and forced me to look up. He moved closer, so close that I could smell his cologne. When our noses touched, my eyes reflexively closed. He kissed me. First, a peck on my lips, and then I felt his tongue slither in my mouth. Although I'd just left the restroom, I wanted to turn and run back because I suddenly had to pee again.

Byron slid his hand around my waist and pulled me closer. His tongue went deeper into my mouth. My eyes opened. I saw him looking at me, so I shut my eyes again. It was the first time I'd ever kissed a boy. I doubt if I was doing it right, but he didn't stop, so I assumed I did alright.

When Byron unleashed my waist, and my weight shifted from the tips of my toes to my heels, I know I looked goofier than I did the day he first asked to copy my homework. I looked to my left and saw Tanya Scully—the biggest gossiper in school—staring at us. Her mouth was opened so wide I could count every tooth, and cavity, she had. Tanya and I were in the same class in that period. Her tardiness often earned her a detention, but on this day, being late for class gave her the inside scoop on a piece of gossip juicy enough to be sold to the National Enquirer.

Tanya darted up the stairs like a child who'd walk in on her parents having sex. On legs that felt like limp noodles, I tried to follow her.

"Aren't you forgetting something?" Byron asked.

"Oh, yeah," I said and grabbed my books.

Before Byron released the books, he said, "Meet me after school by the student parking lot."

I nodded, grabbed my books, and staggered to class. By the time I walked through the classroom door, the chatter had already started. Now I could see the teeth—and cavities—of every pimple-faced student sitting in the room. My popularity rating went from 20 to 100.

The next few weeks were a blur— being identified as Byron's girlfriend took me from the social outhouse to the penthouse. I no longer ate lunch alone. I was no longer the butt of the joke. Underclassmen now looked at me and pointed when I walked down the hallway. One nosey teacher even said, '*A little birdie told me something about you.*' My eyebrows raised in curiosity. Really! Byron and I became so close that I even shared my darkest secret with him. I told Byron that my dad sexually abused me as a child. I don't know why I said it, but I did. His response was sympathetic but barren in the empathy department. How could he be? He was over six-feet tall and weighed close to two hundred pounds. The closest thing to the physical assault he ever experienced was on a football field. Besides, the damage of sexual abuse is more emotional than physical. At seventeen years old, Byron couldn't be much more than a shoulder for me to cry on.

I'm not sure what the tip of Cupid's arrow was laced with, but when it pierced my heart, it left me too love-struck to think straight. I became enveloped in my emotions. Thinking about Byron was as routine as breathing. I was head over heels in love. And like most teenage girls, I feared losing my boyfriend to the hordes of groupies that jostled for his attention. After several discussions, I finally gave in to Byron's subtle but persistent pressure to have sex—my first big mistake.

I stood in our usual meeting spot near the student parking lot and waited for Byron to show up. He arrived fifteen minutes late and saw the frown lines on my forehead as he approached.

"What's up!"

"I've been waiting on you…that's what's up."

"My bad. I got caught up with—"

"Your fans. I know. I saw the way Tanya was all upon you in gym class."

"Tanya ain't nobody to me." He grabbed me by the waist. "You, my baby."

I pushed him away. "That's what we need to talk about."

"What…Tanya?"

"No, Byron." I rubbed my belly and looked at him.

"You hungry?"

"No, Byron!"

"Well, what are you talkin' 'bout?"

"I'm pregnant, Byron!"

Those deep dimples of his vanished like they'd been filled with plaster. He looked around to see if anyone was within earshot and then leaned in. *"Are you sure?"*

"Yes. I took two pregnancy tests."

Byron rubbed his forehead and started to pace. His size twelves dug a trench in the asphalt while he talked —more to himself than me—and scratched his temple. "I've got a dozen scholarship offers. I can't go to college and take care of a baby. If I don't go to college, I ain't gon' make it to the NFL. This gon' mess up my plans."

"No, it's not," I said.

He stopped and looked at me for the first time since I'd told him. "What'cha mean?"

"It ain't gon' mess up your plans because I ain't havin' this baby."

"You gon' get an abortion?"

I looked down at my stomach, my hand still resting near my navel. "I don't want to, but we both know we can't take care of a baby."

Byron didn't protest. I didn't change my mind. Two weeks later…I didn't have a baby.

The warm water was tranquil. I became so relaxed that my body slid down until my mouth was at the water level. My eyes flew open like window blinds. I scooched up so that I wouldn't drown and stared at the evaporating bubbles.

I slid my hand underneath the water and poked around until I touched the loofah. I squeezed out every drop of water and rested the back of my head against the tub again. An image of Byron smiling at me with those pothole sized dimples flashed across my mind.

I wonder what he's doing these days, I thought. *And I wonder what kind of parents we would've been.*

Chapter 2

Dr. Riggio sat behind her massive mahogany desk with her elbows planted on top of it, and her hands elevated to her chin with her fingers interlocked. Her thick silky hair rested on her shoulders and framed her flawless face the way expensive curtains provide the perfect accent to a living room window. The thing that stuck out most to me as I sat in the high back chair across from her were those eyes. They were a beautiful shade of brown and perfectly shaped—as if Michelangelo had carved them. As beautiful as her eyes were, she didn't always use them for good. Their primary purpose was to render you immobile—Medusa style—while she stared into your eyes and unlocked your thoughts. I don't know if it's a trick she learned in college or if it was a God-given talent, but that woman could look into your eyes and examine your soul. It's like she teleported into your mind and walked around inside of your head with a flashlight, searching for the secret you've hidden in the darkest corner.

I've been called a lot of things—primarily stubborn—but I must admit, I repeatedly lost the stare down battle with Dr. Riggio. Like two gunslingers standing ten paces away and facing each other in an old, dusty western street, we locked eyes and didn't blink. But the longer I stared, I could feel her footprints in my head—opening locked doors in search of memories I'd intentionally locked away. So, I looked away to keep her from getting a glimpse of my soul, which was battered and bruised by the disturbing memories that ping-ponged around in my mind since our last meeting.

"Are you okay, Kassidie?"

"Yeah. I'm fine."

Riggio nodded slowly and moved her interlocked fingers from underneath her chin.

"Last week, we discussed some things that left you shaken when you left here. How have the last six days been for you?"

"They've been fine," I said and shrugged. "Work. Home. Netflix. Feed my cat. Same routine...no change."

"Umm-hmm," Riggio muttered and stared at me.

I could tell by her tone that she didn't believe me. I'd have to rely on my ears to discern her disposition because I refused to make eye contact. I looked away like the characters in Greek Mythology who encountered Medusa. Unfortunately, just like those characters that foolishly entered Medusas' lair, I didn't look away fast enough. Riggio had already seen all that she needed to see when I first sat down.

"I've thought a lot about you since last week, Kassidie."

"Isn't that normal?"

"What?"

"You thinkin' about your patients after they leave."

Dr. Riggio rocked back in her seat and sighed. Her fingers were still intertwined, but now they rested in the space below her breast and above her belly.

"It used to be the norm back when I started my career nearly twenty years ago, but I'd be lying to say that's the norm now. A lot of people come to see me for a show."

"For show?"

"Yes. People are usually searching for sympathy from friends and family. My discussions with them are..." she looked around her office as if searching for the word and then looked back at me when she found it, "...a placebo. You know sessions when we haven't discussed anything revealing, but they walk out of here acting like they've been cured. It's all a show—something that they can brag about with their friends while drinking Bloody Marys at brunch." Dr. Riggio stood up. "Those are the sessions I forget after they're done." She walked around the desk, sat on the edge, and crossed her arms. "I got into this line of work because I believe God put me here to help people—people like you, who *really* need someone to talk to."

I heard everything she said, but I focused on the word *really*. It stuck out like she'd sprinkled it with a little cayenne pepper. Was she implying that I was crazier than some of her other clients? I didn't know whether to be flattered or offended.

"Kassidie, I thought about you all week because we reached a point that eluded us for weeks. I was truly frustrated when we ran out of time. If I could've canceled the *placebo treatment* that followed you, I would have. Now, I'm going to ask you a simple question: Did you think about the things you told me during our last meeting?"

I nodded.

"Another question. Did new scenes come to your mind?"

I reluctantly looked at her. I could feel a tear dangling on my eyelash when I said, "Yes."

The leather couch seemed more comfortable. It massaged my back. The headrest caressed my head the way a good hair-washer does at a beauty salon. My eyes closed, and Dr. Riggio's calm tone was as soothing as the sound of John Coltrane's saxophone singing the tune, *Naima*.

"Do you feel relaxed?"

I nodded.

"Good. Now, I want you to think back to our last discussion. Take me to that day; in particular, what happened when your mother returned from the store."

I took in enough air to make my chest rise. When I exhaled, the memories of that evening spilled out of my slightly parted lips.

"Mama came home from the store and made a beeline to the kitchen. My mother, Mary, was a fantastic cook. She knew that her famous spaghetti and meatballs were my favorite meal. Earlier that day, she promised to make it just for me, and when she returned home, she kept her promise.

"I didn't have an appetite that evening. My body ached. I felt like I could still feel my father's fingers probing me like a thousand centipedes running wild on my tiny frame.

'Eat your food, Kassidie,' mama said.

But I couldn't. I just stared at the fork. Body slouched. Eyes glued to my thighs.

'Why aren't you eating?' she asked.

I wanted to tell her so badly. I tried to say to her that I can't eat because my daddy—the man she loved—had just snatched my innocence."

"Was your father at the table?" Dr. Riggio asked; her voice sliced through my thoughts with the precision of a scalpel.

My eyes opened. "Yes, he was."

"What did he do or say?"

"I stole a peek at him and saw his eyes—dark and frightening—looking at me. His eyes said all that his mouth couldn't: *You'd better not say a word.* I was terrified. The man whom I would've run to if I ever felt threatened willingly was now the boogie man, I feared the most.

'Maybe she is not feeling well,' he mumbled and shoved his fork, wrapped in spaghetti and dripping with sauce, into his filthy mouth.

"My mother reached over and placed her hand on my forehead. 'She feels fine. No fever.' I wanted to scream, 'It's not my head that hurts, mama!' But I didn't. Fear has a way of collapsing your windpipe; the way a man with hands the size of my fathers could."

"That's understandable," Dr. Riggio said. "Victims of sexual abuse are often torn between telling the truth and suffering in silence. Kids often display more Emotional IQ than adults. You knew the ramifications of telling your mother what happened."

"I think I was more afraid of devastating her," I said.

"That's the Emotional IQ that I'm speaking of Kassidie. You intuitively knew, even at that young age, that telling your mother what he did to you would turn her world upside down the way your father had just turned yours. In reality, no one would ever be as devastated and impacted as you were—and still are—but children are selfless. You thought about your mother's emotions more than your own."

"He must've known I would."

"He knew how much you loved your mother and was counting on you to put her feelings before your own."

"And I did." I shook my head in frustration. "I should've said something."

"No, Kassidie...your father shouldn't have touched you."

There was a silence that reigned for what seemed like hours before I spoke again. Much to Dr. Riggio's credit, she let me have that moment. Her Emotional IQ was on full display.

"You know what two questions I wrestle with the most?"

"Tell me."

"I often wonder why did my father do that to me? I mean, he was a handsome man. He was tall and strong. I'm sure he could have gotten sex from women around the neighborhood or even from a ten-dollar prostitute. But he chose to violate me—his only child.

"The other day, I was watching television and saw a story about a man who was convicted of molestation. He got ninety-nine years."

"How did that make you feel?"

"My heart sank. For some reason, I started thinking about a pedophile's thought process. What was his method of choosing a victim? Could he tell which kids would run? Was he able to spot the fighters—the ones that would make it hard on him? Did he size up the way a child walks, talk, or interact with him, and then come to his conclusion, 'she or he is the one who will be the easiest?' "I turned off the television and wondered if my father viewed me as someone who wouldn't fight back or run. Did he see me as a weakling?"

"You're not weak, Kassidie," Dr. Riggio said. "You weren't weak back then, maybe physically but not mentally. The fact that you're talking about this now is proof that you are not weak. Your father was a sexual predator. Predators exploit those who are weaker. He outweighed you by two hundred pounds. You were at his mercy."

"Yeah," was the only response I could muster.

"You said there were two questions. What's the other question you are pondering?"

"Honestly, the second question makes me angrier than the first."

"Why?"

"Because deep down, I knew there would never be an answer."

"What's the question?"

I rose from a prone position like a dead person who rises from a casket in a horror movie. Dr. Riggio seemed a little surprised by my change in my body's position. I placed my feet on the floor and rested my elbows on my knees. As I struggled to fight back the tears, I looked up at the good doctor and said, "I often wonder why God would let that happen to me. I was just a child—a child who needed protection, and yet I was a victim of some hideous acts that no child should have to experience from the one they love the most, daddy. *Why?*"

When I got home that afternoon, I didn't feel inclined to hop into the bathtub the way I did the previous week. Instead, I poured myself a glass of wine and plopped down on my couch. I could see Dr. Riggio's face after I revealed the second question. It was the first time I'd ever seen her flustered. That second question will do that to you. If a psychiatrist, who has seen and heard it all during her twenty-year career, can be stumped, then it's no surprise that myself—and countless others—have wrestled with that question.

Sure, I thought about seeking an answer from spiritual advisors, but what do they know? Their default is always those clichés we've all heard over the years: *The Lord moves in mysterious ways,* or *Only*

God knows; we just have to trust in Him. Translation—they don't have a clue.

I finished off my glass of wine and stretched out on the sofa. As my eyes closed, I pondered that age-old question that no one can answer: *Why me God?*

Chapter 3

Zero patience. That's what I had while darting in and out of I-75 traffic, trying to make it to my five o'clock appointment with Dr. Riggio. Road rage had never been my thing, but from the moment I spoke of being sexually abused, I became angry. Jay-walk in front of my car—tongue lashing. Eyeball me too long— get mean mugged. Cut me off in traffic—a mandatory two-mile tailgate. I was becoming the very person I once despised, and I didn't understand why.

Dr. Riggio was already waiting in her counseling chair when I barged through her office door, breathing as I'd just finished a marathon. A glass coffee cup, with a tea bag string dangling over its rim, hovered around her lips. I could see the red bottoms of her stilettos as the setting sun tossed a ray through the fifth-floor window. It collided with the diamonds in the bezel of her Cartier wristwatch and temporarily blinded me. She wore my money like a biker wears a tattoo, *I thought*. Considering my willingness to flirt with vehicular homicide to make it to her office on time, I'd say she earned every dime that went into her wardrobe.

"I'm sorry, I'm late."

Dr. Riggio studied me while sipping her drink. She placed the cup down, and without uttering a word, waved in the direction of the sofa. Her silence made me feel small. I avoided eye contact and scurried to the couch as a child scolded for taking a cookie from the cookie jar.

"The traffic was terrible. I nearly had a wreck and got into two arguments. What's worse is that I was at fault both times. I don't know what's gotten into me lately. It's like I have a chip on my shoulder the size of a bolder. I've never been like that." Realizing

I'd been rambling, I paused to allow her to chime in. She didn't, so I continued. "Can I be honest?"

Dr. Riggio nodded slightly and placed her elbows on the arms of her chair. She placed her hands in front of her face—the tips of her index fingers touching her bottom lip—and studied my every move.

"I didn't start acting this way until I told you about the abuse. It's like that confession unlocked a wave of anger that I can't control. Everyone I encounter is starting to look like my enemy."

"Hurt people...*hurt* people."

Four words. Four measly words were all it took to open my emotional flood gates. Wisdom, sautéed in the perfect pitch, can have that effect. Within seconds of hearing those simple words, I was curled up on that sofa in the fetal position with the *ugly cry* face.

"Kassidie," she whispered, "I need you to dig deep and find your strength. You can do this."

Her words were soothing and penetrating. Like a seasoned cornerman imploring a boxer to get off the canvas before the referee's count reached ten, Dr. Riggio's words grew arms, straightened my contorted frame, and lifted my head.

Once I was upright, she walked over to her refrigerator and returned with an ice-cold bottle of water. I believed Dr. Riggio cared. But I'm not stupid, I wasn't the first emotional wreck she counseled, and I wouldn't be her last. She'd mastered the art of being supportive and heavy-handed all at once. Allowing me to release my emotions was important, but it was also vital for me to complete my purge and make progress within the allotted one-hour time period—no such thing as overtime on a shrink's couch.

I ripped off the cap and took a swig, spilling a little on my shirt. The cold water sent a jolt through my system like jumper cables on a dead battery.

"Are you okay?"

I nodded.

Dr. Riggio gestured for me to put the bottle on the coffee table. I followed her direction and assumed my normal, prone counseling position.

"How old were you when your parents divorced?"

The question caught me off guard. I was expecting some type of counseling foreplay, but she decided to dive right in.

"I was around seven. Umm, I guess you can say it messed me up."

"What do you mean?"

"It left me confused."

"The fact that your parents got a divorce confused you?"

"No, that didn't surprise me. Even though I was a child, I knew my *papa was a rolling stone*. He was an Army man, tall, strong, smart, and ruggedly handsome. Based on some of the arguments I used to overhear, he and my mother had, he had a mistress in every port he touched down in."

"So, what was it about the situation that left you confused?"

"Well, considering what he'd done to me, you would think I'd be ready for him to go away. And at times, I was. But like I said, I was only seven years old, and as much as I feared him, I also loved him."

"You can hate the pain someone causes you and not hate that person."

"Tell me about it," I said sarcastically. "For a long time, I felt like my father was the only person whose funeral would be a sad and joyous occasion for me."

"When your parents divorced, did you tell your mother what happened?"

"No. I wanted to, but once again, I became conflicted. It was like a part of me wanted to give my daddy the benefit of the doubt. He touched me repeatedly, so it wasn't a mistake, but I could not bring myself to tell my mother."

"Tell me about your relationship with your mother."

"What do you want to know?"

"Were you close to her then? Are the two of you close now?"

I thought long and hard about the question before answering. I'd never been forced to examine my relationship with my mother. From my perspective, she'd never been the source of my problems, so it was a road I never ventured down. But, with Dr. Riggio studying me like I was a lab rat and the reality that I was paying her to analyze my emotions, money that I couldn't get back, I felt compelled to search the corners of my mind for a reply.

"Umm, we had a good relationship as a child. We have a good relationship now. I love my mother, and I know she loves me."

"Does she tell you?"

"Tell me what?"

"Does she tell you that she loves you? Was it common for her to say those words when you were growing up?"

"My mom has never been the type just to toss the phrase, 'I love you,' around. Don't get me wrong, she said it, but she was the type of person to show her affection more than talk about it. Honestly, I'm not sure if she was capable of being that type of mother when I was younger."

"Why do you say that?"

"Because she was only a child herself. My mother had me when she was fifteen. She was a child herself. I don't believe she was emotionally evolved enough to understand the importance of articulating her feelings. Now that I'm an adult, I understand the importance of telling the people you love how you feel about them. I probably overdo it with my children. I didn't get that type of verbal affirmation as a child, but I knew she loved me. Mama is different. Even to this day, she's stingy with the word *love*. It's just the way she is."

Dr. Riggio was quiet, but I could hear her ballpoint pen against the paper. I peeked over at her and saw her head down as she scribbled feverishly.

She looked up and asked, "Did your parents have joint custody?"

"Honestly, I don't know what their arrangement was. All I can tell you is my daddy moved to Houston and got remarried. I must've been around nine years old."

"Did you visit him in Houston?"

Immediately, I could feel my chest rise and collapse as a sigh that felt like it originated in my heels spilled out of my mouth. While staring at the panels on the ceiling, I was debating whether to tell her what happened between my father and me after his move to Houston. Before I could come to a decision, Dr. Riggio offered one of her trademark gentle nudges.

"Holding back will only keep you in emotional bondage."

My lips pressed together reflexively, my body's attempt to corral my words. But that pain had taken up residence in my psyche for too long. It was time to issue an eviction notice.

"Yes, I would go visit him during the summer."

Honestly, my mother never liked me going to visit my dad—I guess she kind of sensed something wasn't right. She would always hastily pack my bags the week before school let out. I don't blame her; she was unknowingly sending me to the enemy's camp. *She never knew what was happening.*

Anyway, I would stay with my dad every summer after they divorced. From the moment I stepped on their front porch, it was awkward."

"Why is that?"

"Because my stepmother, JoAnne, wasn't feelin' me. During that first summer visit, I learned the difference between being tolerated and accepted. Acceptance has a distinctive look: long talks, laughter that comes from the belly, girl outings—the little things that make it clear to a child that she's not an unwanted accessory."

"Well put. And how did *tolerance* look to you back then?"

"The same way it looks to me now: short responses, no eye contact, being annoyed by the little things, and only showing an interest when the person you're trying to impress is around. That's how JoAnne made me feel."

I propped up on my elbow and grabbed the bottle of water. While I guzzled, Dr. Riggio took the opportunity to sip some of her tea.

"Tell me what happened between you and your father during the summer visits."

"The sexual abuse went to another level. My dad didn't forcibly attack me. He began to do subtle things like exposing himself."

"What do you mean?" Dr. Riggio placed her cup down and grabbed her pen and notepad.

"As I said, JoAnne didn't like me. So, she would leave the house a lot and be gone for hours. I guess out shopping or something. Honestly, I believe she was just trying to stay away from me for as long as she could.

While she was gone, my dad would walk around the house wearing a robe with no underwear on, and he'd sit down and position his body so that his...his..."

"Take your time," Dr. Riggio encouraged.

"While I sat on the floor and watched television, he would sit in this high-back chair that was off to my left and position his body so that I could see his penis." I paused to wipe a tear that broke free and raced down the side of my cheek. My eyes zeroed in on a crease in one of the ceiling tiles. By focusing on the zig-zag pattern of the crease, I was able to keep my thoughts from racing and focus on the story I was telling. "I didn't want to look, so I locked my eyes on the television – while noticing him in my peripheral view."

"The sexual acts would start subtle. It's how child abusers test boundaries. He'd already touched you while he was married to your mother and got away with it, *right*. In a different setting, there were new variables for him to factor in. For example, exposing himself was the beginning stage to gauging how far he could go with you in that new environment."

"I suppose so. Eventually, I stopped sitting on the floor. I figured that if I relocated, he couldn't expose himself to me, but that didn't work because things went from bad to worse."

"How so?"

"I was too young just to leave the house, and even if I could, I didn't know anyone in the neighborhood. So, I would go and hide in the den closet. "Why the closet?" "It was the only safe place I could find because he would never look for me there.

I would ask to go outside to play with some of the kids up the street. At times he would let me – and sometimes he wouldn't. The screen door used to squeak and smack the door frame whenever you opened and closed it. I would open it and let the screen door slam shut. And then I would sneak back into the house and hide in the closet. Sometimes, I would even fall asleep in the closet.

"One day, I noticed a box filled with Playboy and Hustler magazines. I was curious as to why the books were tucked away in an unused closet. Like clockwork, later that evening, after we finished eating dinner, JoAnne left my dad and me at the dining table, grabbed her purse and hit the door. When we were alone, he asked, *'Did you look at Daddy's magazines that were in that closet?'* Of course, I denied it the way any child would. He gave me a stern look as if I was not telling the truth. But he didn't yell at me. He smirked and said, 'I don't mind you lookin' at them, but don't tell JoAnne. It will be our little secret.'"

"Maybe the magazines were planted in the closet," Dr. Riggio said. "Another test of your boundaries."

"Well, I got *tested* that entire summer and each summer after that. I badly wanted to tell my mother not to send me to his house for the Summer, but I couldn't. Because if I did, I would've had to tell the whole story of why and what was happening, so I had to wipe away my invisible tears and go.

"My dad lived near the airport. Back then, you could park near the end of the runway and watch the planes take off. I loved watching the planes take off — we drove out there a lot. Imagine being seven, eight, nine years old, and watching the airplanes lift-off while wondering, *where are they going?* —it was a fantastic feeling.

"One day, he insisted on teaching me how to drive. I was around eleven and didn't understand why I needed to learn how to drive. The idea of driving was cool, and I was excited, so I said 'okay.' Until he placed me on his lap to navigate the steering wheel, and I felt his erect penis. I pretended not to notice. That went on for the first few "lessons." Eventually, the lesson became dreadful because of his perversion going further. One day, after the driving lessons ended, we drove to the airport to watch the planes take off. It was there it happened openly, 'he pulled it out and exposed himself and said touch it,' I knew *exactly* what he meant.

The silent tears begin to stream down my face. I was afraid, afraid to show my real tears.

Nevertheless, "I didn't see the planes take off that day." Dr. Riggio, it is hard to look up when you're forced to look down."

The drive home from my counseling session that day was a stark cry from my journey to it. I drove in the slow lane, dazed in my thoughts. This lane is where getting lost in your dreams are supposed to be allowed. Apparently, I was lost in a black hole, engulfed in my feelings to the point that even the other right lane daydreamers were getting annoyed. They honked, cursed, and flipped me the bird so many times that it seemed like a gesture of endearment.

It took a phone call from my husband to snap me out of my trance.

"Hey babe, I've been trying to reach you. Where you been?"

"Hey, I umm…I had some errands to run after work."

"Where are you now?"

"Downtown. I'm stuck in traffic."

"Where are you headed?"

"Umm, I'm headed back to the office. I've got to finish this report before tomorrow morning."

"It's been like this for the past few weeks. Every Thursday, you've got to work late. Look, I'm not accusing you of anything, but I've gotta ask…is there something you need to tell me?"

Yeah, the moment you left the country, I started seeing a shrink, I thought.

"No, baby, I don't have anything to tell you. Things have been busy at work. Dealing with the type of people I deal with, and their problems can be draining. You know that."

"I've told you to work on detaching yourself from it all. That stress is going to eat at you. It can even make you sick."

"I know, honey. I'm working on getting better at that."

An agonizing sigh that had become all too familiar seeped from his mouth and slithered through the phone line right before he said, "Kassidie, I miss you."

"I miss you too, honey. I promise I'm fine. Just be safe over there and call me tomorrow."

"I will. Love you."

"I love you too," I said and hung up before he could ask anything else. Hiding the fact that I was in counseling seemed wrong, but I felt I needed to. It was my baggage that I needed to unpack—on my own time and terms.

After we hung up, I sank back into my emotional abyss. I continued to drive below the speed limit in the right lane on I-75 for the next twenty miles, oblivious to the world outside of my car, but aware of the dysfunction riding shotgun next to me.

Chapter 4

Once I started seeing Dr. Riggio, my relationship with sleep eroded. Whenever I tried to rest, my eyelids would fly open like the creepy lids on a ventriloquist's dummy. Wide awake, I'd remain until *sleep* brought his butt back around at three in the morning: clawing at the door like a puppy trying to come back inside after relieving himself. For six straight nights, I stared at the ceiling, hoping I get enough rest to combat the anxiety and stress that seemed to have me in a chokehold. A glass of wine before bed didn't work. ZzzQuil didn't work. Even counting sheep failed to get the job done on time. When my eyes finally closed and I'd get close to sniffing that elusive REM sleep, my alarm clock would squeal like a stuck pig.

By the time I arrived at Dr. Riggio's office for our next meeting, I was an agitated insomniac eager to vent. I plopped down on her couch, ready to get started—no small talk or foreplay—just a woman in need of a release.

To her credit, Dr. Riggio rode my energy like a surfer catching a wave. She grabbed her notepad and tea and slid into her comfy chair, ready to ask the question that would unleash the beast lurking inside of me.

"Kassidie, tell me about the last time your father took advantage of you."

"I remember it like it was yesterday," I blurted out. "I was twelve years old. It was the summer before I started the eighth grade. I was so excited about entering the last year of middle school that I remember pleading with my mother to let me stay at home that summer. But she didn't. 'Your father has been bugging me about letting you come to Houston. He wants you to see his new house, she told me. I couldn't have cared less about seeing his house.' I knew the new home wouldn't change his old habits. Here I was again faced with the anticipation of wanting to tell her why I didn't want to go, but I just couldn't build up the nerve to say it out loud."

"I must admit, the house was gorgeous. Two-story. Large backyard. Manicured lawns up and down the block. The area looked like something out of a Norman Rockwell painting—the American Dream on full display. But for me, the dream was a nightmare that I couldn't escape.

"From the first night I arrived, the abuse started, and every night after, sometime after one o'clock in the morning, he would tiptoe down the hallway into my sisters' bedroom.

Dr. Riggio interrupted, and asked 'why your sister's room?' Because I slept on the floor in her bedroom."

"Ummm, Okay, *continue…*"

My stepmother always went to bed early, so the house was dead silent. The only creature stirring was the six-three predator whom I called *daddy*.

"I'd pretend to be asleep when he entered my bedroom, but that didn't stop him from exploring my innocent body and touching me since I slept on the floor, I guess, so he didn't disturb my sister. I wonder now, whose idea was it for me to sleep on the floor?

"Why?"

"I don't know. I guess because it was convenient to walk into the room quietly and discreetly as if checking on my safety like any father should while hovering over me like a tall black tower."

"*He probably wanted you on the floor to keep the bed from squeaking and making noises.*"

"Maybe so. Either that or he thought his wife might come in and see him bent over the bed looking under the yellow blanket that covered me. All I know is to this day; I avoid sleeping on the edge of the bed. When I would do sleepovers at my friend's house, I called for the bed and intentionally left my sleeping bag at home." I sighed and continued.

"One time, I was sleeping on the floor, and I heard his footsteps as he walked down the hallway. He walked in and knelt beside me.

He thought I was sleep, but honestly, I never slept during the visits because I always wondered, *is he coming tonight or not?'* He came in, knelt beside me, and pulled the blanket down below my thighs to expose my panties. And proceeded to do the unthinkable...”

“Did you ever cry or yell?”

“No. Truth be told, as time went on, my eyes stopped producing tears. I became lifeless and numb to it all, like a storefront mannequin—stiff and desensitized. One thing that did result from the traumatic experiences was that I developed an unhealthy fear of sleeping in a dark room. To this day, I sleep with a light on.”

“Your stepmother never suspected anything?”

“No, I don’t suspect she knew anything, but if she did, she didn’t let on. Do you remember Cracker Jacks—the caramel popcorn?”

“Yes.”

“Do you remember as a kid, eating the popcorn with the anticipation to—”

“Getting the prize inside of the box,” Dr. Riggio interjected and smirked.

“Yes. Eventually, you’d get around to the popcorn, but it was the prize that mattered the most. I used to dig in the Cracker Jack box like a dog hunting for a buried bone. That’s how my stepmother made me feel—like the Cracker Jack popcorn. My dad was the prize she wanted; I was something she tolerated to have him.”

“I know that must have been hurtful as well.”

“I guess so. The thing I took from it was that I had no one to tell my problems to, so I buried them deep inside, making it hard for me to remember. I often thought my mother had no idea what was going on behind my dad’s four walls, and my stepmother was either too emotionally disconnected to notice or willfully ignorant so that she could have plausible denial. Either way, I was a twelve-year-old and forced to live in a silent world with noise all around me. Not being able to talk to anyone still affects me to this day.”

"I agree. Let's try and stay focused on the last incident. Please continue."

"By the end of that summer, my body was transforming, body parts that were flat started to bloom. Whenever I would go to the neighborhood store, boys who appeared to be in their late teens would stare at me like I was their peer. Of course, my dad noticed the changes also."

"What do you mean?" Dr. Riggio asked and moved the tissue box closer to me so I could reach it. I declined with a head shake—I needed to feel the tears on my cheeks because, for so long, I hid them behind my eyes.

"It was hot that summer. I'm talking close to one hundred degrees every day. The humidity was unbearable. Puberty was in full effect, and the moisture from the heat felt like fire on my skin. My stepmother would always tell me I smelled like *outside,* and point at the bathroom. Then she would go on her daily excursions—never bothering to invite me—and leave me with my dad.

"By mid-summer, I was taking two showers daily. One day, after I got out of the shower, I noticed a mirror sliding under the bathroom door."

"A mirror?"

"Yes, a mirror. I guess he was trying to see me naked. I moved closer to the bathtub to get out of the mirror's view, and this went on for two or three days straight. Until…"

"Until what?"

The memory of my next confession grabbed me by the throat. It was as if some unseen force was determined to keep my truth trapped inside.

"This is a safe place, Kassidie. You can release your pain here. Tell me what happened."

"I…I was in the bathroom. I got in the shower, but I must've forgotten to lock the bathroom door. My father came into the bathroom. Naked. He stepped in the shower with me."

Suddenly, I needed the tissue that Dr. Riggio offered. "Everything is black from that point on. I honestly can't remember anything after that."

"That's enough for today," Dr. Riggio said and placed her note pad on the coffee table.

I sat up on the couch and cried because I walked in her office that day, determined to be strong as I talked about my past without the waterworks. But there I was thirty minutes into our session, an emotional basket case. I was sobbing uncontrollably, like a little girl who'd just found her favorite doll beheaded.

Dr. Riggio slid her eyeglasses to the bridge of her pointy nose and watched me for a few moments. After studying me, she did something that she hadn't done with me before. She glided over to the couch and sat next to me. The touch of her hand and the scent of her expensive perfume were soothing. She draped her arms around me and pulled me close. Her embrace served as the cocoon I needed at that moment to feel safe.

"I know this is hard," she whispered. "You've shown a lot of courage, young lady."

"I want to tell you more, but I can't...I just can't remember. I know more happened, but..."

"Shhh, ...it's okay. At times memory loss is your brain protecting you. Being able to keep traumatic memories, locked away, is admirable. You should be proud of yourself." She grabbed my chin and forced me to look into her eyes. "I'm proud of you, Kassidie."

"Thank you," I mumbled.

"I think we've covered enough of the abuse for today. Next week, I want to focus on how the abuse you suffered has impacted your decision making as an adult. That will help us identify harmful patterns. Once we do that, we can move on to figuring out a strategy for coping with your past. Is that okay with you?"

Too choked up to speak, I agreed with a nod. Perfect timing is what Dr. Riggio had. Her suggestion of moving toward a coping strategy was a lifeline because the tides of pain were rising, and with each rehashed memory, I could feel myself getting closer to drowning.

The Transition

"*Stop the mindless wishing that things would be different. Rather than wasting time and emotional and spiritual energy in explaining why we don't have what we want, we can start to pursue other ways to get it.*"

~ Greg Anderson

Chapter 5

I left my counseling session feeling physically and mentally exhausted. My hair looked like I tried to comb it with a pitchfork. The business suit I wore was wrinkled, indications of crying and slobbering shown clearly on the jacket sleeve. Starting my car was a task. My energy level was as low as a superhero character who uses their powers to save the world. The plan for the evening was to grab some shrimp fried rice on the way home, wash it down with a glass or two of Stella Rosa Black wine, and try to find a Netflix movie that was entertaining enough to keep me from drifting into a coma-like sleep.

I made a stop by Market Street near my house because they carried my favorite brand of wine. The parking lot was packed, so I had to park the equivalent of a football field from the entrance. I outmaneuvered a monster truck driver for the space at the end of the parking lot. He flipped me the middle finger and showered me with a few words that no man should ever direct at a woman, but I moseyed along like I didn't notice him.

I continued walking alongside a string of retail shops. Their tall windows inviting pedestrians to look inside, I stood between the grocery store entrance looking inside the nail salon and yogurt shop. But quickly, my attention was redirected to something going on inside the pizza parlor that made me stop in my tracks. Two middle-aged men, dressed in red polo-style shirts and khaki Dockers, were holding on to a teenaged black boy. The boy looked like a wishbone that is seconds away from being broken into two pieces, as the men clung to his flailing arms.

I stood outside that pizzeria with my mouth open, and my eyes glued to the three of them like they were wildlife, and I was a spectator at the zoo. Customers parted like the Red Sea as the men drugged the young man out of the store and pinned him against the wall. Moments later, two security guards, one with ketchup stains on his shirt, the other wore a shirt with missing buttons, pulled up on a golf cart.

"Is this him?" asked one security officer.

"Yes. We caught him this time," said one of the store employees.

"The police are on their way," said the second security officer.

The store employees released their grip and returned to the store. The teenager looked like he had a mind to run, but I stared into his eyes and mouthed, *'Don't do it.'* My words must have spoken to his spirit because he sat on the window ledge and awaited his fate.

"May I ask what he did?" I asked.

The security officers looked at me and said in unison, "Credit card fraud."

I moved along at a much slower pace. As I walked down the grocery store aisles, I had a reoccurring thought: *What kind of daddy issues did he have?*

"Seems like you're in a much better mood since the last time I saw you."

Dr. Riggio supported her light-hearted observation with a sly smile. Considering how snot poured from my nose during our last session like Viola Davis' nose in any movie she plays in, I appreciated her attempt to remove any embarrassment I may have felt.

"Yeah, I'm doing much better," I said and sat down on the couch. "Sorry about the waterworks."

"What waterworks?" she asked and winked. "Water? Tea?"

"You know what, I'll take a cup of tea today."

"One lemon tea coming up."

My host sprang to her feet, enthusiastically. I'd been her patient for six months. The first two months consisted of me sitting across from her with my arms crossed, not bothering to hide the fact that I didn't want to be there. I was like most black people who assume that counseling is a "white thing." But, during the last four visits, I had diarrhea of the mouth. My icy exterior had thawed. My willingness to accept a drink was another sign of my trust.

I drank the tea slowly. My body twitched as the warm liquid trickled down my throat. The scent of lemon opened my nostrils. I felt alive.

"At the end of our last meeting, I told you we'd spent enough time talking about the effects of your sexual abuse experience. I believe I have a clear picture of what all went on. I'd like to spend today's session talking about the aftermath of the abuse. In many cases, kids who suffer from sexual abuse trauma act out. Talk to me about your life after the last time he sexually abused you."

I took another sip of my tea to calm my nerves. I placed my cup on the coffee table and started to lie down, but Dr. Riggio stopped me.

"Please remain sitting upright. To move to this next stage— past the abuse—I want you to sit up and talk to me. This upright posture is symbolic of your transition."

I wasn't quite sure of what she meant, but it *sounded* reasonable, so I obliged.

"Well," I said and exhaled, "the summer with the shower incident was the last time I went to visit my father. I suspect that my mother instinctively felt like something was not right, so she didn't push the issue when I told her I didn't want to visit my dad. My stepmother never wanted me to come, so she didn't insist when I didn't ask to visit anymore. I suspect my father was starting to get nervous about me talking, so he didn't put up a fight either."

"Did you act out?"

"Are you asking if I was promiscuous?"

"Yes."

"No. I know it seems like that would be the natural response for victims, but it wasn't for me. I didn't become the teenage girl that slept with any boy who flirted with me. As a matter of fact, I was withdrawn, shy, and quiet. I mean, I wasn't a hermit or anything; I had friends. But my trust issues made it hard for me to be close to anyone. I kissed a few boys and eventually lost my virginity, but it was forgettable. I believe I laid there like a wet blanket. It was like I was empty of emotions throughout my teen years."

"I understand. When people go through traumatic experiences, their response is to either adopt or detest the behavior. The victim can either repeat the cycle of abuse or be a faithful advocate against sexual abuse."

"Considering the foundation that I've opened to help victims of sexual abuse, I guess it's obvious which route I took." I shook my head as my thoughts drifted back to the young boy whom I witnessed taken into police custody. "I may not have turned to sex, but I went through my rebellious phase."

"What did that look like?"

"The other day, I saw a young boy getting arrested for credit card abuse. My immediate thought was, what kind of *daddy issues* he had."

"Sometimes, PTSD can be triggered by a sound, smell, or something we see. What was it about that scene that made you reflect on your daddy issues?"

"I was arrested for credit card abuse as a teen."

Dr. Riggio's eyebrows arched.

"I know...I don't look like the type."

"I know there isn't a *look* per se, but I wouldn't have guessed that you were once involved in any kind of criminal activity, let alone, arrested."

"Yep. I had my share of trouble," I said and shrugged. "I was young when it happened." My head shook up and down while I spoke. "I'm so ashamed to admit that I did it—it was completely out of my character. I mean, I never got in trouble in school. I never got detention or suspended. Honestly, most of my teachers barely knew I was in class while in high school."

"Continue."

"I just sort of fell into it. A credit card came in my mail one day. You know, back in the '90s, they didn't have all of the checks and balance systems as they do now. It was a lot easier to use a credit card that wasn't yours. I thought to myself at the time, *Use it. Who would know?* So, I opened the envelope and saw a Neiman Marcus logo, and my eyes got as big as the headlights on the front of a truck.

"I knew I should have tossed it or given it back to the mailman, but I didn't. My spirit was talking to me, but I was young, naïve, and unwise. I went shopping. I tried to use the card at a Neiman Marcus in town to buy a dress for church on Sunday—*go figure*. The card got declined. The sales lady didn't take the card. She just told me the sale wouldn't go through. The Lord was giving me a chance to stop, but I still didn't listen. What do you think I did?"

"You went to another Neiman Marcus store," said, Dr. Riggio.

"Yep," I said and shook my head in disgust. "I had an overwhelming feeling like I just needed that dress. Looking back now, I can see that it was my ego and greed. Truth be told, it may have even been my pride—I'd lost my innocence; I suppose I felt like I needed to control something—anything. But, my actions are not an excuse for being hurt."

I believe Dr. Riggio agreed with me on that last point because she nodded.

"I found that same dress at the second store I went to and headed straight to the register. The saleswoman swiped the card and then looked at me strangely. She said, 'Wait here one moment.' I remember feeling nervous. I could sense something was wrong. Suddenly, that dress that I *had* to have didn't matter. I said, 'That's okay. I'll come back.' When she didn't stop, I knew I was in trouble."

"What did you do?"

"I left that dress right there on the counter and walked toward the exit as fast as I could without breaking into a sprint. Right as

I made it through the crowd and reached the double glass exit doors, the undercover security guard grabbed my shoulder. Thirty minutes later, I was in the back of a police car."

"That must have been an experience."

"It was the worst. Because it happened during the weekend, the process of bailing someone out is slower. By the time my mother and stepfather came to get me, I was already wearing the orange jumpsuit."

"Did your mother call your father?"

"No. By that time, my dealings with my dad were next to none, and because I was a young adult, my mother had no reason to talk to him anymore. She and my stepdad handled it. To this day, I don't think my dad knew about the incident."

Dr. Riggio started scribbling in her notepad. I waited until she finished writing and continued telling the story.

"I'll tell you what, those couple of days that I spent in the jail scared me straight. Imagine being surrounded by women who treated being in jail like it was no big deal. I mean, they laughed, joked, and braided each other's hair like they were at a backyard barbeque. For me…I couldn't take it. I climbed on that top bunk and cried so hard that my eyes were swollen shut by the time my mother arrived to bail me out.

"The dress I attempted to buy with that card was on sale for less than two hundred dollars, and that was the first time I'd *ever* been arrested in my life, but the judge didn't show me any mercy. After lecturing to me for what seemed like hours, he gave me ten years' probation."

"Ten years? It seems a bit excessive."

"Not only did I get ten years' probation, but I also had to stay at the jail for thirty days every weekday night, go to work on my regular civilian job—which was at a bank—and then return before eight o'clock at night. I don't even know if they still do stuff like that, but that's what happened to me."

"It's funny you should mention the word excessive because it took a few years for me to have a trial. By that time, I was in my twenties and working for a very prominent African-American attorney. I mean, this man was sharp. He would always challenge me to do more with my life. I highly admired and respected him."

"When I received a court date, I was terrified. I built up the courage to tell him about my case. He listened and didn't say much when it was time for me to go to court; he voluntarily represented me, and the charges got dismissed. He didn't charge me a dime. Instead, he challenged me to do something with my life."

"Why do you think he did that?"

"I guess he saw something in me."

Dr. Riggio nodded in agreement. "You were a young woman trapped in emotional purgatory. Your mother was a teenage mother. Your father dysfunctional, possibly a victim of abuse himself. You were the only thing that kept them tethered together. But you were also the person in that equation who received the least amount of *right* attention."

"You think using the credit card was my attempt to get attention?"

"I'm saying, displaced aggression can appear in different forms. It's impossible to have all that pent-up anger, and it not show in some form or fashion. You were angry at your father. You couldn't tell your mother. So, you took it out on some faceless person."

"Makes sense," I muttered. "I must've got all of that anger out because I never did anything like that again. From that point, I became obsessed with changing my life and completing my education. Over the next fifteen years, I earned five degrees— including my doctorate."

Dr. Riggio sipped her tea and then moved the cup from her lips. She smiled and said, "As I said, displaced aggression can appear in different forms like promiscuity, repeat abuse…" she took another sip and then smiled and said, "…or in the pursuit of enough education to show those who preyed on you that you're more than a target."

Chapter 6

My counseling sessions with Dr. Riggio were cathartic in and outside of her office. After each session, I often went home and thought about what we discussed for hours.

I wondered if I'd left anything out—information that might have helped her better understand my past and my reaction to being sexually abused as a child.

The discussion about my arrest stuck with me. It was a time in my life that I've tried to suppress and shove deep into the back of my mind. If I could have a do-over, I would. But there are no do-overs in life. You learn from your mistakes and live with the consequences of your actions. I believe I've done a good job at that, but it doesn't mean the memories of my transgressions don't haunt me.

I was shocked to discover my confession of pride — and the need to control things — actually came out of my mouth. I wasn't aware that being sexually abused hurt me as much psychologically as it did physically. Sexual abuse takes an emotional toll on the victims more than people will ever understand. *Physical, emotional, and psychological*, I was bruised in all three areas. I often wonder which area was damaged the most. If I had to choose, I'd probably pick the emotional part of me. In my late teens and early twenties, my heart was a black hole. Feelings went in, but they rarely came back out.

Some people turn to the liquor bottle to mask the hurt. Some turn to illegal drugs or prescription medication to numb the pain. My mother was a religious woman who raised me in a traditional Baptist church. She took me to church faithfully—no pun intended. I accepted Jesus Christ as my Savior at a very young age. But, like most children, paying attention to the Pastor was often a challenge. Whether it was staring at a cute boy in another pew or someone struggling to stay awake, my focus on getting the *word* wasn't always there.

Nevertheless, I did learn enough about the grace and mercy of God to push me to reconnect to my relationship with my Savior, especially after my life's hardships. Proverbs 22:6 says: *Train up a child in the way he should go, and when he is old, he will not depart from it.* It was time for me to return to my foundation. I surrendered to God and rerouted my life back to where it all began, on the Word of God.

Reconnecting to my spiritual foundation started in the summer of 2002 when I met Jack. We had a strange relationship because we only talked about God. He was a nice-looking guy, but he never tried to engage in a relationship with me. It was as if God allowed our paths to cross so that I could witness a man who was genuinely concerned about my spiritual walk with Christ.

Jack and I would spend hours on the phone. Talking about the life of a believer and what it meant to live a life, according to Romans 12:1, *I appeal to you, therefore, brothers, by the mercies of God, to present your bodies as a living sacrifice, holy and acceptable to God, which is your spiritual worship.*

One night, in particular, stands out to me. Jack called me around 1:00 am and spoke in a whisper, 'Turn on your T.V., to the Trinity Broadcast Network,' and quickly hung up the phone. I grabbed my remote and turned to TBN, and a lady was speaking by the name, Prophetess Juanita Bynum. She was sharing her testimony titled, *No More Sheets!* That was life-changing for me. Bynum's message was powerful. She was ministering on fornication, I grabbed my Bible and turned to and began reading, 1 Corinthians 6:18-20: [18] *Flee fornication. Every sin that a man doeth is without the body, but he that committeth fornication sinneth against his own body.* [19] *What? Know ye not that your body is the temple of the Holy Ghost [which is] in you, which ye have of God, and ye are not your own?* [20] *For ye are bought with a price: therefore, glorify God in your body and in your spirit, which are God's.*

WOW! Late in the midnight hour, I rededicated my life to God in the middle of my bedroom floor, I wanted and needed to surrender my whole life again. It became difficult trying to reestablish a relationship with God and living the way I was.

Being newly single and living life the way most single women do, I dated and even had a *"friend with benefits"* named Quentin. Whereas Jack was a *spiritual* friend, Quentin was my *sexual* friend that stimulated me mentally, intellectually, and physically. I already had my own home and a good job, so the one thing Quentin could provide was physical. He was older, intelligent, attentive, and aggressive, and I couldn't imagine not keeping him around for those purposes.

Jack was a constant voice in my ear and always called at what seemed like the right time. He ministered to me about life, relationships, and God. I now know that God was dealing with me internally about fornication, and it was becoming a *real* conviction. So much so, that sex with Quentin was no longer enjoyable.

One Sunday morning, I chose not to visit my home church and visited a good friend's church. When I entered the church, it was a different crowd than what I had been used to in my church. There was a spirit of liberty. I felt the presence of God from the time I entered the doors. When the Pastor took the microphone, he spoke boldly and said, *'I do not know who I'm talking to right now, but fornication is wrong. No matter how you look at it, it is wrong.'*

Those words hit me right in the core of my gut, like a punch from Mike Tyson. I fell to the floor and cried like a baby. I cried out to the Lord, *"I'm sorry! I'm so sorry, God, Why! Why didn't anyone tell me I was wrong, God! Why!"*

My emotional outburst lasted the whole service. I couldn't control myself. It was as if a weight had lifted from my body. Yes, Jack had introduced me to Prophetess Juanita Bynum ministry, and I knew God—but I had never felt the conviction of my sins. That was a refreshing time for me because my eyes were open, *for real*. I knew there was a change on the inside of me. That day was one time I will never forget. My body felt limp by the time service ended. I went home and began to evaluate my life, relationships, and the next steps I would take.

The first order of business was to deal with Quentin, but we needed to have a conversation about our relationship, so I invited him over. We sat on my couch, and I could feel my emotions swirling in my stomach of nervousness.

Let's pull the band-aid right off, *"we need to stop having sex,"* I blurted out. "I'm at a place in my life that I now want a relationship that doesn't involve sex."

Quentin stared at me as if he was waiting for me to say, I'm just joking. When my facial expression didn't change, he knew I was serious.

"What brought this on? Why are you deciding now to stop sex?"

"Honestly, I want to try this new relationship with you, but I understand if you don't want to do this. We can still be friends. The difference is, if you stay overnight, you're going to have to sleep on the couch."

Quentin agreed to go along with the new relationship parameters. At least he pretended to be okay with the relationship. The truth has a way of coming out. It wasn't long before he started asking to have sex again. I believe he thought I was going through a phase and would give in eventually, but I held my ground.

A few weeks passed, and Quentin called me. *"I can't be in a sexless relationship,"* he said. He was as convicted as I was about my new lifestyle, and I wasn't mad at him. I understood.

Okay, is all I said — hung up the phone. It was the last time we spoke.

My life had transitioned from existing to living. I left my church home and moved my membership to Faith Walk COGIC and served there for the next five years.

As for Jack, he just phased out of my life like the sunset. It was if he came in just to redirect me, and when God's plan was complete, he was gone. I've often thought about him over the years, but we haven't spoken again since that final late-night call.

When Forgiveness Comes

"Forgiveness liberates the soul, it removes fear. That's why it's such a powerful weapon."

~ Nelson Mandela

Chapter 7

There are two certainties in life, death and taxes—*for me*, there are three, death, taxes, and the moment you decide to change your life; often, the areas you choose to change are the ones that will test your faith.

I was determined to abstain from sex after my relationship with Quentin ended. I focused on studying the Bible and trying to make sure that the steps I took were in alignment with God's word. That was my top priority. Before Quentin, my life in sin was considered acceptable according to society's standards. And by the time I was thirty years old, I'd been in two serious relationships.

I was, divorced with two kids, which was not a part of *my* plan. However, there is an old saying: *adversity doesn't build character; it reveals character.* My children are blessings from God, and loving them is a privilege. Yes, being the primary caregiver for two children was hard, and mommy duties don't stop just because you have to punch a time clock. Being present and available for my kids was intentional even when I was too tired to take care of myself. The mandate will send people into an emotional tailspin, but it did the opposite to me—my children became my motivators!

The desire to provide a better life for my kids motivated me to improve my quality of life.

It was as if I had an out-of-body experience that allowed me to see myself in the third person—I wasn't pleased. I was doing an excellent job of raising my kids, but I wasn't working on growing myself professionally, emotionally, educationally, and, most important, spiritually. God had more in store for me, and I knew it. By the time that out-of-body experience was over, my mindset of procrastination shifted.

I began to align my life and focused on my goals, and the desire to get the best education became my priority. Doing the work was never a problem for me; I love learning. However, avoiding the mental potholes that littered my path to success was a major weak spot for me. All it took was one bad dream or the sight of something that triggered a bad memory, and my desire to do anything other than curl up into a ball and be alone would reappear.

I understood the importance of putting God first, but trying to win the emotional battle on my own was losing ground. It wasn't until I recommitted to my spiritual walk, the potholes that once tripped me up became filled, and my journey to educational achievement became easier.

I wrote my goals down in my journal, along with my favorite scripture, Jeremiah 29:11—and finishing my college education was at the top of the list.

The first stop on my road to "becoming educated" was returning to Valley College (VC). Ironically, this is the lowest degree I have, but in many ways, it was the hardest one to earn. Being a mother of two children, I worked a fulltime job and became a fulltime student. Nevertheless, I was determined to walk faithfully toward my destiny. My mother and stepfather were the foundation of my support team. They often kept my children so that I could attend night classes. I persevered and pushed through to complete my first degree, an Associates' Degree in Science in two years.

Isaac Newton's first law of motion states that an object that is at rest will stay at rest unless a force acts upon it, and once in motion, it will not change its velocity unless a force acts upon it. For years, I was that object that was at rest, but completing my associate degree created a momentum that would not be slowed down or altered by any force. When I graduated from VC, I immediately enrolled at Baptist University (BU) and began working on my Bachelor's in Communications and Christian Ministry.

My time at BU was transformational because of the Christian curriculum, as well as the spiritual environment, which fostered a desire to begin my emotional healing while getting my education.

While sitting in the parking lot of BU listening to Shekinah Glory's worship song, *Yes*, I begin to cry uncontrollably. The tears streamed down my cheeks, like, a rogue storm can drench an otherwise perfect picnic. While crying, I glanced at the rearview mirror, noticing the clarity of my tears, and they appeared as clear as fresh river water. Instantly I felt a strong presence over me, and my soul felt refreshingly renewed. I felt alive again. I was reminded of (John 7:38), *"Anyone who believes in me may come and drink! For the Scriptures declare, 'Rivers of living water will flow from his heart.'"*

I was in a vulnerable place with the Lord, and I knew I wanted all that He had ordained for my life according to (Jeremiah 1:5), *"I knew you before I formed you in your mother's womb. Before you were born, I set you apart and appointed you as my prophet to the nations."*

Yes, my life's journey had been turbulent and shattered into pieces. My mentor told me once, *"that God would sprinkle the exact measure of grace needed for each season in your life."* In that season of my life, God truly gave me the Grace I needed to continue my educational journey. The word *yes* was forever etched in my heart. I was not going to return to what God had delivered me from, my feet point forward, and that was the direction I choose to go.

The next six years were fruitful. I completed my bachelor's degree and moved immediately into the graduate program to earn a Master's in Christian Education and Christian Counseling. You would think that was enough, but God said *no*, keep going. The momentum was too strong; I moved effortlessly right into my second graduate degree program and earned a Master's in Business Administration in Management.

While earning my MBA, my ability to see my future had become crystal clear, I was focused entirely on doing God's will, raising my kids, and serving the people in His kingdom. My soul still said, *yes!* The mind is like a rubber band; once it has stretched, it can never go back to its original form. The day when I stood draped in my graduation regalia and started to flip the tassel on my graduation cap from right to left, signaling another completed degree, I was grateful that God could love me like this, despite my mess!

Sure, the road was hard at times, but I continued to grind it out. When you get out of the way and allow God to direct your footsteps, you become secure in your faith. You know that regardless of what turns and detours you may encounter along the way, one thing for sure is when you walk in the footprints of Jesus, you will arrive at each destination.

After having tackled and conquered my education, it was time to embark on another professional journey. I wanted to reclaim all the devil thought he had stolen from me during the first part of my life. Genesis 50: 20, states: *'You intended to harm me, but God intended it all for good. He brought me to this position so I could save the lives of many people.'*

With that scripture serving as my new fuel, I snatched back the control of my self-esteem and became determined to be an advocate for others. I opened my non-profit organization, Life After Advocacy Group, Inc., where the mission is to advocate for victims of sexual abuse. *'A loud voice for the silent voice!'* I was on fire and excited all in one.

At this point, I'm sure it is no surprise to you to hear me say that opening my business was another challenge. Sometimes your funds and your ideas aren't on the same page. That can cause a delay. The time you spend away from your kids: business meetings, conferences, client interaction, can damage your ability to be an attentive parent. Not being able to be the type of hands-on parent you'd like to be at their school activities, falling asleep while promising to watch a movie with them. Even opting for fast food instead of cooking the hot meal you know they need. I went through all of that, and I am not ashamed of it. I'm also not ashamed to say that when God sees you are committed to your goals, He will make a way, out of, no way. He will stiff-arm bitterness and resentment like a running back shedding a would-be tackler so the loving bond between you and your kids will remain secure. He will provide money, which is nowhere to be found when you need it, but always appear when the lights get cut off. Or when the inflexible jerk you encountered during negotiations is miraculously replaced by a more understanding individual. Believe me, when I say, as it pertained to my business, God made—and has continued to make—a way out of no way.

There was a time in my life when money was next to nothing. One night while driving home from a business meeting with only twenty dollars to my name, for pampers and a McDonald's meal for the kids, I sat at a red light and glanced to my left, there stood a panhandler asking for money. Honestly, I acted like he was not there and began to hurry the light in my head when it changed – I hit the gas pedal hard. *Whoa!* I said.

When I turned the corner, the Spirit of the Lord said, turn around and go back to give him the money – WHAT? My car slowed down as I approached the next light in heavy thought, *'how am I going to buy pampers, how am I going to buy food?'* I said, okay Lord, made a U-turn, still thinking if he is gone GREAT, at least I was obedient! Nope, he was standing there. I rolled down my window, passed him the money, and said, *'be blessed in the Lord.'* Long story short, I picked up my kids, went home, checked my mailbox, and there was a $200 check addressed to me! God will provide when we obey!

In the life of the *believer,* we walk on rocky roads and have to make a conscientious decision to stand straight—because the darts in life are thrown right at us to test our strength, faith, and belief. God is amazing!

Life was moving fast. I had sleighed the education dragon and conquered the fear of starting my own business. I felt accomplished but alone - after divorcing my first husband, releasing the wrong relationships, and no sex for ten years…that's right ten years. I abstained and put Jesus first. Raising my children, serving in ministry, ministering the Gospel, and bringing awareness and prevention to sexual abuse, assault, rape, and molestation became my primary focus. Still, God designed us to have our emotional needs met. The desire to share our lives with someone equally yoked is natural. No matter how much I tried to ignore my need for companionship and intimacy, I couldn't shake it.

I began to pray for the man I wanted and needed in my life. Someone I could be comfortable with and who would compliment me. Before surrendering to my calling, I made 'the list' of qualities I wanted in a man. All the superficial stuff: a good job, nice car, handsome, straight teeth, tall, chocolate brown—things that were devoid of substance. Whether or not he was a Christian was camouflaged by his external makeup. Once I got my spiritual house in order, my list of "must-haves" in a man changed too and became non-negotiables. I wanted the man that God had for me because of what I was doing did not work.

I choose to wait on God to send me the right person. The man of my dreams needed to have a personal relationship with God, prayed, and insisted on praying for us, and love my children. Too many times, people treat children from previous relationships like the extra pack of soy sauce that comes with your Chinese food—just thrown-in. My children are not a "throw-in." We were a package deal. Any man that wanted me needed to prove to me that he wanted to love my kids too. My vow to abstain from sex was a serious one, and my future husband would need to be willing to respect my choice to wait until marriage. I wanted a spirit-filled and Godly man—not a boy. The type of man I wanted would understand and embrace the responsibility that comes with living a life of servitude.

Those were my non-negotiables, and I made no apologies for them. There was no need to waver or worry because I knew that God would give me the desires of my heart as long as I was in His will (Psalm 20:4) KJV, *"May He grant you according to your heart's desire, And fulfill all your purpose."*

As with most things in life, the moment you let go and let God, those things you seek come to you. God's time is not our time. I stopped staring at my "must-have" list as the words would somehow combine and create a perfect man that would leap off the page and into my life. I prayed on it and let it be—and wouldn't you know it—my search for the right man ended.

A friend of mine introduced me to my current husband. With my reservation, I let down my guard and opened up to the process. We began by spending hours talking on the phone, getting to know each other's goals, expectations, values, and spiritual foundation. Our conversation was great! I'm talking the "pick it up on the first ring" kind of good. He was kind. Respectful. Inquired about my kids just as much as he did me. You never get a second chance to make a first impression, and he didn't need one. His grade was an *A*, which wasn't an easy grade to earn because, at that stage in my life, I was a tough grader.

In courtship, there is always a moment when the man will do or say something that will either seal the deal or send a glaring red flag – signaling he is not the one for you. *The signs are always there.* Unfortunately, when your "must-have" list is a list filled with superficial things, your vision is blurry, and your judgment is impaired. I gave God my list, so I knew I didn't have to be paranoid about identifying faux pas and hiccups. I could relax and enjoy the journey because I knew God *had me.*

He was honest upfront and firmly stated, *'I am looking for a wife, not a girlfriend.'* I thought my ears were echoing back at me, that I stuck my finger in my ear like a Q-tip—no wax. My hearing was fine. I asked him to repeat that, and he did it again, but this time with sincerity, *'I am looking for a wife, not a girlfriend.'* I clutched my imaginary pearls and tried my hardest not to sound excited. I pulled it off, but my emotions were breakdancing inside of my body. In hindsight, I should have got an Oscar for that performance. Rather than work on a long drawn out acceptance speech, I just held the phone to my ear and smiled while peeking up at the ceiling and mouthing, *Thank you, God!*

The process was going great! I needed confirmation. So, I surprised him with a visit and arranged dinner at one of my favorite restaurants. It was time for me to see if he was indeed my husband, I needed to sit in his presence to discern if he was the one for me.

Yes, the word tells us in Proverbs 18:22; *"He who finds a wife finds what is good and receives favor from the LORD."* However, God speaks to both the man and woman, *so* as I need confirmation too.

We sat and talked as freely as we did on the phone. I was being Inspector Gadget and watching every little detail about him. His table manners were on a little rusty, but okay. He didn't hold the cutlery like a Neanderthal, and he didn't chew with his mouth open. He was the same kind, soft-spoken, and caring person who displayed the love of God just like he did on the phone. He asked questions about my kids, which tugged my heart because they were not generic questions that any faker would ask, but intuitive and caring questions. He reminded me of things I'd mentioned about my kids that I'd forgotten about, and honestly, I didn't realize he had taken notice. He was quick to offer suggestions on how to deal with a teenage boy, and not just nod his head reflexively. The waitress was bringing out dessert, and he glanced over at me and asked, 'when are their birthdays?' I couldn't believe what I was hearing. I mentioned my kids' birthdays during those first "feeling out" conversations three months earlier. He remembered. It wasn't his responsibility to recall that small but essential detail, *but he did.* That small gesture—to go along with the other qualities that I'd already observed—let me know that he knew *how* to love my children and me, the deal was sealed. I knew for sure he was the one.

Approximately ninety-days after we met, he proposed to me. I'm not ashamed to admit that I didn't waste any time accepting his proposal. I didn't start dancing in the streets, but I had a smile on my face so wide that the corners of my mouth tickled my earlobes.

Shortly after the proposal, we enrolled in pre-marital counseling. It was during those sessions that I revealed to my fiancé that my father had sexually abused me as a child. I needed to know if he could understand from a spiritual place, the pain, loss, and emotional damage that comes from being a victim of sexual abuse. Not only was it necessary that he understood, but I also needed to know if he could deal with it—those are two different things.

The man of my dreams sat quietly and allowed me the space to talk through the tracks of the abuse. I didn't hold anything back. Every disgusting detail revealed. However, the more I spoke, the more I noticed his body language change. The vein on his forehead started pulsating. I could see the muscles in his forearm twitch. Pressed lips told me all that he wanted to verbalize but felt compelled to suppress. When urged by the counseling Pastor to share his feeling, he just kept repeating aloud that he couldn't understand how someone could sexually abuse their daughter. His reaction didn't anger me. Truth be told, I was pleased by it. A man who doesn't care about you enough to become outraged by the actions you suffered from the abuse, probably won't have the emotional IQ to identify—and be a helpmate—when your past is causing problems for you in the present.

The longer I talked about my abuse, the more questions he had—How did it happen? Where did it happen? What did your mother say? What happened to your dad? I expected to get bombarded with those questions, but once they began to come like a dart thrown at a dartboard, I could feel myself losing it emotionally. My palms became clammy, and my hands shook. My sentences became choppy, and pools of water formed in my eyes.

Right when I started to wonder if my confession had torpedoed our marriage plans, I noticed his expression change. The frown lines that aligned his forehead vanished. His lips eased and were no longer tightly pressed together. His fist went from being balled to holding and caressing my shaking hands. The compassion I knew was inside of him was made clear to me at that very moment.

Exactly eleven months after the day he proposed, we got married. For those of you reading this book, you may be wondering—if we abstained from sex until our wedding night. *Yes*, it was part of the *no* in both of our spirits. There was no need for a *trial run* before the wedding night because we knew God had bonded us together, and He doesn't make mistakes. We knew He (God) had synced us together, and our first time would be perfect—and it was.

Chapter 8

f the stormy weather was any indication of the type of session
with Dr. Riggio that awaited, then I was going to need enough
Kleenex to fill a shopping cart. The rain that covered the city
created driving conditions so poor that traffic on I-75 crept along
at a school zone pace. I feared I was driving through a tornado.
Turning around and going home was an option, but my time in her
office had become so cathartic that the fear of being swept away in
the gushing wind became secondary.

I arrived nearly fifteen minutes late. When I walked in, Dr.
Riggio was at her desk, sifting through notes in the pad she often
scribbled on. I entered and sat down like a child reporting to the
principal.

"Sorry, I'm late," I said and sat on the couch with my knees
pressed together and my hands atop them to keep them from
knocking. "That weather is terrible. I nearly had two accidents."

"Yeah, it's bad out there, but I knew you were coming," Dr.
Riggio said and smiled. "Do you know why I'm smiling?"

"Not really," I replied, wondering if it was some type of trick
question.

"I'm smiling because that lets me know you are committed
to the healing of process. If you were only interested, I would
have gotten a message from my assistant saying you'd canceled."
She moved to the chair she routinely sat while listening to me
babble about my past. "I'm proud of you. You should be proud
of yourself."

Dr. Riggio was as smooth as they come. Her words were as
soothing as a grandmother's and as convincing as a slick-talking
pimp. By the time she draped one leg over the other and looked
into my eyes, I was ready to spill my guts—heck, that woman had

me so wrapped around her finger that I would've run a few errands for her in the rain.

"We've lost some time due to the rain, so let's get started."

I was about to lie down but stopped when I saw her head shake.

"No, no, no. I told you, we're past that, no more laying on your back to tell me about your past. We are now in the present—clarity, and resolution. You are the beauty that has risen from the ashes. Let's get prepared to fly."

I smiled and glanced at my arms to see if I was developing wings.

"Okay. Where do you want me to start?"

"I want you to tell me about the day you finally told someone what happened to you."

"Well, the first person I told was the woman I babysat for as a teenager."

Dr. Riggio leaned back in the chair and placed her index finger against her temple. With squinted eyes and a raised brow, she urged me to continue.

"When I was pregnant with my son, I still visited the woman whose kids I babysat as a teenager. We developed a relationship over the years. One night, she and her husband were about to go to dinner. I stopped by to say hi. As she was getting ready—touching up her makeup and hair—I sat on the bed. She was looking in her bedroom mirror and must've noticed I appeared down because she asked, 'Is everything okay?' I'm not sure why my past was weighing so heavily on me that night, but it was. I couldn't hide my emotions. So, I sat there and told her everything that happened to me."

"What did she say?"

"She mainly listened. I mean, what could she say? It's hard to give someone advice on this type of situation if you've never gone through it. The one thing she did encourage me to do is tell my mother what happened."

"Did you follow her advice?"

"Yes. Reluctantly, but I did finally build up the nerve to tell my mother what my father had done to me when I was a child."

"That must've been hard for you."

"You have no idea." At that moment, there was a flash of lighting outside of her office window and a thunderous clap that made me flinch. I could feel tears the size of those raindrops forming in my eyes, so I snatched some tissue from the box on the coffee table. "Dr. Riggio...telling my mother what happened to me was one of the scariest moments in my life."

Dr. Riggio nodded in agreement. "I bet it was. Tell me what happened?"

"I went to her office. My mother worked at a finance company. She was a loan processor, so she had her own office. When I showed up at her office unannounced, I could see the look of surprise on her face. It only took a few seconds before that look morphed into concern. I rarely went to her place of work at all, let alone without giving her a heads-up."

'Mama, I need to talk to you about something,' I said.

'Kassidie, what's wrong?' she asked.

'Are you sick?'

'No,' I said. 'Maybe emotionally sick, but not physically.'

"She closed her office door and then sat down. I sat in the chair in front of her desk.

'Baby, what's wrong?'

'I don't know how to say this...'

"She cut me off."

'Just say it, baby. Whatever it is, we can get through it.'

'My dad used to touch me when I was a child.'

"My mother's bottom jaw nearly hit the floor. It was clear that she wasn't expecting to hear that, I suspect she would have preferred to hear that I was sick. At least sickness can be dealt with—fixed. But the way her eyes grew twice their normal size, it was apparent she was not prepared."

'When did this happen?' she asked.

'It started when I was six years old. One time you went to the supermarket and left me home with dad. I was watching *Good Times* when you left. He took me into the bedroom and…'

"I stopped talking when I saw my mother's hand rise and cover her mouth. I'm not sure if she was trying to stifle a scream, but it shook violently as her emotions bubbled up and unleashed."

'I remember that day,' she mumbled.

"Her eyes, repeatably shifted from me and down at her desk while she spoke as if she was the only person in the room."

'Oh my God, I remember that day. When I came home from the store, I made spaghetti—that was your favorite meal. You didn't eat much. You just sat there quietly. I kept asking you if you were okay, but you didn't say anything. I should have known.'

"A tear broke free and streaked down her chin."

'I'm your mother—I should have known.'

"I joined her in a silent cry. I stared at my legs, too ashamed to look up at her."

'That's when it started,' I continued. 'That's why I never wanted to visit dad during the summer. He would wait until JoAnne wasn't around, and he'd expose himself and sneak into my bedroom every night. He would…'

"My mother's second hand flew up. She used them both to cover her mouth. I supposed the desire to scream had become too great."

'I don't need to hear anymore,' she said.

"She reached across her desk and held out her hand until I grabbed it."

'Baby, I'm sorry. I'm so, so, sorry.'

"I'm not sure what I expected her to do with that information, but after we sat there in silence for a moment, she did what any mother would do—she spun in her chair and grabbed the phone. Once she started dialing, I knew all hell was about to break loose.

"I could only hear one side of the conversation, but based on her remarks, I knew he did what most fathers accused of sexual abuse would do—he denied it."

'Hello, Kellen, this Mary. We need to talk NOW!'

There was a pause, and then she lit into him.

'Kassidie just told me that you sexually abused her as a child. She said you touched her inappropriately as far back as when she was six years old. She said you did it whenever she came to your house during the summer.'

There was an even longer pause. I could hear my father talking, but his words were coming out through the receiver in a distorted fashion. My mother stood up.

'You're a damn liar!'

I was too afraid to move, but I wanted to make sure my mother's office door was closed. My head turned one hundred eighty degrees like a child possessed by the devil in a horror film. Thank God it was. The last thing I wanted was *our* business to be overheard by a gossiping coworker.

'Why would she make something like this up, Kellen? Why?'

"My mother's face scrunched. She held the receiver in one hand and crossed the other arm over her chest."

'Kassidie has never been the type of child to hound you for money. And you're not going to make believe she's making all of this up because you wouldn't give her some damn money. You're still the same lying dog that you've always been. Stay away from my child!'

"Mama slammed the phone down. It landed so hard in the cradle I thought it would crumble into a million pieces, but it didn't. I can't say the same for my mother's heart. She plopped down in the chair and started crying uncontrollably. So much so that I had to go over and had to console her. I believe she felt guilty for not seeing what was happening right under her nose."

"It's not uncommon for the parent who didn't see the abuse to feel like a failure," Dr. Riggio said.

I nodded in agreement. "She and my stepdad had kids. My real dad and JoAnne had two kids. I often felt like I was the lone ranger—trapped between two families, sort of the forgotten child." I guess that's why I kept everything that happened to me, bottled up for so long. I've always had this fear of ruining everyone else's world, while my world was crumbling around me."

"Did they ever talk again?"

"Not for a long time. I believe my mom wanted me to hate him as much as she did, but I couldn't back then, and I still don't." I studied Dr. Riggio for a moment to see if she would comment on my confession, but she didn't. "I know I should. I know it may sound crazy that I don't, but it's the truth. Once I became spiritually grounded and understood the true meaning and importance of forgiveness, I could no longer remain mad at my father for what he did to me. I forgave him." I shrugged and leaned backward until my back touched the sofa. Once my mother saw that I forgave him, she eventually forgave him too.

"What about your husband?"

"My husband is a very laid-back man. He is slow to anger. When I told him about the things that my father did to me, he was in disbelief. He couldn't wrap his brain around how a man could do that stuff to a child, let alone his child. *Anyway*, they have a cordial relationship. They aren't the best of friends, but they get along."

Dr. Riggio started scribbling in her notes. When she finished scribbling, she looked at me and asked, "Did you tell your children what happened between you and your father?"

"No, I didn't just sit them down and tell them the story, but I did tell them in phases. As they grew older—my daughter now a college student, and my son is out on his own—they can understand better all that happened."

"Does your father have a relationship with them now?"

"My son is very reserved; whatever feelings he has about the situation he has kept to himself. They get along fine. My daughter loves her grandfather, but she does keep her distance. She was bothered by what she learned, but she still loves him. They've always had a good relationship."

Dr. Riggio's head tilted the way a dog tilts his head when trying to understand the weird human talking to her.

"I guess I should go back to clear some things up," I said. With my elbows on my knees and my fingers interlocked, I tried to fill in the gaps. "What I mean by *always* is that when my dad came back into my life, he bonded with her."

"I don't quite follow you."

"Let me explain. A few years ago, my dad got divorced from JoAnne. He lost everything in the divorce and moved from Houston to Dallas."

"Was it because of what he did to you?" Dr. Riggio asked.

I could feel a wave of heat rush from my torso up to my neck. I knew my response would garner a side-eye glance from her.

"It wasn't because of what he did to me. They got divorced because he molested her niece."

"I'm not surprised," Dr. Riggio said. "That predatorial instinct doesn't just go away. When you were no longer available, he targeted someone else." She jotted down a few notes and then asked, "Did he go to jail?"

"I'm not sure. I don't believe he knows that I know about the situation. A cousin of mine told me what happened. My dad has never mentioned to me about what happened that lead to his divorce."

"How did it make you feel when you learned that he had molested his ex-wife's niece?"

"I felt remorseful. I wished that JoAnne had believed me when my mom called and confronted him that day. Maybe if JoAnne wouldn't have believed his lie, she may have left him sooner, and that young girl might not have had to experience the terror of being molested. Honestly, I can't say that I felt guilty back then or even today. Is that wrong?"

"You had no way of knowing whether he would have stopped. The truth of the matter is, you don't know when he started molesting the girl. Kassidie, you can only control how you handle your situation and address the emotions you're battling."

"Can I have something to drink?"

"Sure. Water or tea?"

"Water, please."

Dr. Riggio went to the refrigerator. I needed that break to harness my emotions. I felt so naked at that point in the session. My lips were so dry I could feel them splitting. I couldn't get the water bottle to my mouth fast enough. Before I could swallow the water in my mouth, she hit me with another question.

"Knowing that he's a registered sex offender, you still allowed him to have a relationship with your daughter. Why?"

My eyes scanned her office as if an answer would appear in the form of a message on the wall, and it didn't. The answer to that question isn't etched on a wall or appears as a slogan on a t-shirt or coffee mug; it's the type of response that only God can give because it's etched in your heart.

"I allowed him to have a relationship with my daughter because I decided to forgive him without the *but.*"

I expected Dr. Riggio to roll her eyes, call me an "idiot," and then toss me out of her office, but she didn't. All I got from her was silence and a blank stare. It was the type of non-response that forces you to search for more words even when you think you've run out.

"I know it doesn't make sense," I said hesitantly, "but the way I see it, if I was going to forgive him, I couldn't do it with my hang-ups. Forgiveness is for the individual—Let me be clear; forgiveness doesn't mean *forgetfulness.* I remembered everything that he did to me, so I allowed him to come back around and spend time with my kids, but I paid close attention to his actions. It wasn't until…"

"It wasn't until, what?"

"…he started displaying some of the same tendencies with my daughter that he did with me when I was a child."

"Such as?"

"He started asking to spend more time with her alone and wanting to take her places. When I noticed those things, it brought back all those bad memories. I immediately put a stop to all contact with her."

SEEING BEYOND THE SHATTERED GLASS

Dr. Riggio looked at her wristwatch. "Time flies," she said. "It took us six months, but we got here."

"Where is *here*?" I asked.

"The place where you are ready to confront your father."

"Why do I need to do that, I've already forgiven him?"

"That may be true. But Kassidie, I'm telling you what I know... there needs to be a face-to-face between you and your father. You set the time, place, and date, and then express how you feel to him. I believe you need closure."

Chapter 9

For two weeks after my last session with Dr. Riggio, I pondered on her suggestion to have a heart-to-heart discussion with my father about the abuse he did to me as a child. I sat on the topic like a bird on her eggs—letting it incubate in my mind—until I built up the nerve to reach out to him. After much thought, I decided to leave it alone. I'd forgiven my father and going back down that road just didn't make much sense to me.

A few weeks after I decided to move on, I was asked by a colleague to be her special guest at a Women's conference in Nashville, Tennessee. I jumped at the opportunity. Nashville is a lovely city, one of the places I've longed to live, so I didn't have to think twice about accepting her invitation. I would've taken the offer if it had been in a place as boring as Pocatello, Idaho. I was getting cabin fever being stuck at home while my husband was on the other side of the world, and my kids were out living their best lives.

While I packed my suitcase, I also packed away the thought of speaking to my father about the sexual abuse. One thing I've learned in life is that there is no need to force any issues. When a *thing* is supposed to happen—regardless if it's something we are running toward or away from—it will happen in God's time, not ours, which was why I wasn't surprised when I got a phone call from my father.

When I saw the word "Dad" flash on my cellphone screen, I smirked and looked up at the ceiling. *Really, God,* I thought. *I haven't heard from my father in weeks, and you have him call today.*

"Hey daddy," I answered with my phone wedged in the crook of my neck while I sifted through dresses in my closet. "What's up?"

"Nothing much. I was just calling to see what you're doing."

"I'm packing to go to Nashville."

"I didn't know you were going to Nashville."

"Neither did I until three days ago. It was a surprise invitation. I should've started packing yesterday, but I procrastinated."

"When do you leave?"

"My flight leaves at 2 o'clock. I didn't eat breakfast, and I'm starving. I'm going to grab an early lunch on my way to the airport. I figure if I leave within the next thirty minutes, I can eat without rushing and still make it to the airport by noon. I wanna be there at least two hours before takeoff, no telling how long the security line is going to be."

"True."

There was an awkward pause after he replied. I could feel the seconds slipping away from me, and although I wasn't looking to rush him off the phone, I didn't have a desire to hold it like two teenagers struggling to find something to talk about.

"You okay?" I asked.

"Yeah, I'm fine. Umm, you mind if I join you?"

"In Nashville?"

"No, while you eat. I'm kind of hungry too. I can meet you wherever you're going."

To say I was surprised by his suggestion was an understatement. My dad never offered to have lunch or any other type of meal with me.

"Cool," I said because I didn't know what else to say. "I'm thinking about grabbing something to eat at Black Walnut Cafe. The one a few miles from the airport."

"I know the one. Let's see; it's close to ten now. How 'bout we meet at around ten-thirty."

"That'll work," I said. "I'll see you there."

Black Walnut Café was just as I expected it to be at that time of morning—quiet and no long lines to slow me down. I arrived at ten-thirty sharp. I spotted my dad sitting at one of the booths in the corner of the place. He waved at me like I was Mariah Carey, and he was a star-struck fan. After ordering my food and getting my drink, I made my way to the booth.

"How long have you been here?" I asked while hugging him.

"Not even five minutes."

"Did you order?"

"No."

"I thought you were hungry."

"I kind of lost my appetite. I'm just going to sip on this coffee until it comes back."

He fidgeted like a junkie going through withdrawals. The coffee in his cup was nearly at the rim, so he clearly hadn't done much sipping. After a few peeks over his shoulder, he finally made eye contact with me.

"How you doing?" he asked.

"Umm, as good as I was when we spoke on the phone thirty minutes ago." I looked at his trembling hands. The coffee spilled over the rim when he tried to lift his cup. "Are you okay?"

"I'm good. Why?"

"You seem a little jumpy."

"Naw, I'm good." He looked over at the register. "Give me your receipt. I'll go get your food."

I gave him the receipt and watched him walk away. Something was wrong. Based on the paranoid way he was acting, something was very wrong.

He did something. Whatever it is, he knows that it's about to catch up with him. He still doesn't know that I know he molested JoAnne's niece. Did he do the same thing to someone else?

86

"Here you go," he said and sat down. "I brought you a fork and knife."

I studied him for a moment. If shame were a person, it would be easy to spot. It avoids contact, has poor posture, and can't speak without stuttering. The man sitting across from me wasn't named, Shame, but they knew each other.

After saying my grace, I looked right into his eyes. "I have about twenty to twenty-five minutes to eat this and head to the airport. Are you going to tell me what's really on your mind?"

He sipped his coffee, which I assumed was cold by that point and managed to speak to me without looking down at the table.

"I just want to apologize to you," he said, sounding dejected.

"For what?"

"For all the things I did to you when you were a child. I shouldn't have done that to you. If I could take it all back, I would."

The words *"for all those things"* resonated with me. Not because there were, in fact, a lot of things that he'd done to me, but because instead of listing the actual infractions, he went the safer route. The devil tried his best to fuel any attitude within me with those words *"for all those things,"* but not today, Satan! Proverbs 15:18 says, *A hot-tempered person stirs up conflict, but the one who is patient calms a quarrel.*

While my father struggled to get his words right, I started on my meal. Carving my chicken and coupling it with a piece of the fluffy waffle beside it.

"We can't change the past. Trust me. I would if I could. But I can't. All I can do is try not to make the same mistakes." He took in a deep breath and let it out. "I guess what I'm trying to say to you is that I want to ask you to forgive me."

I swallowed my food, took a sip of my tea, and placed my fork down on the plate. I leaned back and placed my hands on the table. We looked like two shooters in an old western staring at each other at a poker table, each considering going for our weapon. I wasn't timid or dismissive by not responding right away. In hindsight, I think I was just taking it all in.

Oftentimes, it's the person that was hurt who ends up chasing the person who hurt them. Begging and badgering the guilty party for an overdue confrontation and lobbying for an apology that usually never comes. I was happy that he apologized, but even more than that, I was glad to see that God touched my father's heart to the point that he felt compelled to ask me for forgiveness.

"Daddy," I said in a voice designed to be calming, "I forgave you a long time ago."

I reached out and grabbed my father's hand; I didn't take another bite of my food. I didn't need to. At that moment, my soul was full. And that was indeed all I needed.

The flight time from Dallas to Nashville is approximately two hours. That was more than enough time for me to process what had just transpired between my father and me, and still have time to get a little sleep before the plane landed.

The person sitting next to me was a teenage girl who wasted no time shoving earbuds in her ear. Before the plane could take off, she'd coiled into a tight ball in her seat—knees pressed against her seat, the hood of her sweatshirt shrouding her head, which rested against the airplane window. That was fine with me because the last thing I wanted at that moment was to engage in conversation with someone who didn't know when to be quiet.

I noticed the person sitting across the aisle from me was reading a novel. The man next to her pulled out his laptop and began pecking away even before the light came on, signaling it was okay to get up and move around. By the time the plane was floating thirty thousand feet in the air and a bed of clouds so white and fluffy they looked like cotton balls, I started to relax and process all that happened at lunch.

He apologized to me, I thought. *That is the first time he's ever apologized for what he did.*

The flight attendant offered a bag of peanuts and soda, so I accepted and battled with a series of questions that fluttered around my head. *Does he have health problems? Why did he choose now to ask for forgiveness? Should I have pressed him to explain to me why he sexually abused me, his daughter?*

As I often do when I'm feeling overwhelmed, I reached for the one thing that I know will give me answers—my Bible. Romans 15:1 states, *"We who are strong have an obligation to bear with the failings of the weak, and not to pleasure ourselves."*

Although scorn might seem like the appropriate state of being when looking into the eyes of the person who sexually abused you, all I felt was sorrow for the man sitting across from me. His sins were eating away at him like maggots eat dead flesh—the inability to look into my eyes for more than a few seconds. The slumped shoulders. The choppy speech patterns. The lack of appetite. My father—the man who was my first example of how a man should act—was mentally, emotionally, and spiritually defeated.

By the time the pilot instructed his crew to prepare for landing, I'd already placed my Bible back inside my purse and was resting peacefully. The girl next to me, who'd slept the entire flight, awakened and slid back the door on the window so she could lookout. A beam of light burst through and sprayed my face. At first, I squinted and turned my head, but once my eyes adjusted, I looked out the window and saw one of the most beautiful scenes ever. The sun appeared to be resting on one of those puffy clouds. For, as far as the eyes could see, the clouds were illuminated by the sun rays.

"Beautiful, ain't it?" asked the girl.

"Yes, it is," I replied.

There is nothing more important in life than having peace of mind. As I soared through the sky inside of a metal bird with God's sun rays beaming in my face and my father's apology still ringing in my ears, I completely understood the meaning of having *perfect peace.*

My Life After

"The struggle has no hold on the outcome."

~ Dr. Ketra L. Davenport-King

Epilogue

It's natural for someone who has gone through what I, and so many other victims of sexual abuse and molestation, have gone through. To ask yourself the question, Why me? Is it a fair question to ask? Sure. Just as appropriate as it is to ask: Why does God allow babies to be born addicted to crack? Why would God choose me to go through this? Was I born to be sexually abused? Did God do to me what he did to Job—was this my test of faithfulness? If God is love, why would He allow an innocent child to be a victim of an act that will scar her for life? There are questions in life that are never going to get answered. I don't care how well versed in scripture your pastor is. No one has the answers to those questions.

One day, while sitting in my quiet place, the question arose, "*Why me?*" It was a passing thought that raced across my mind like a comet. I turned on the television intending to channel surf when the distortion vanished, and the picture became clear, a thick-haired brunette stood there holding a black microphone with red and black numbers identifying channel 8 news. Wind gusts forced strands of her hair to dance, while she said: "Breaking news! A man convicted of molesting a nine-year-old girl was sentenced today to 10-years in prison. His victim was too young to be interviewed on camera, but they quoted her statement, '*He said if I told anyone, he'd come back and hurt me.*'"

My heart started racing. I dropped the remote like it was on fire. Suddenly, an anger that had been lying dormant within me bubbled like lava. It surged through my body and spilled from my mouth. "*Why, Lord?*" I muttered. "Why do you let children continually be sexually abused? Molested? Raped? Beaten until death?

The roof didn't split wide enough, so the heavens weren't revealed. There was no roaring thunder outside of my window. The television didn't flicker and display an image of Jesus, answering my question. Nope. It was just me and my question—alone, with no answer.

Although I didn't get an answer from God, it doesn't stop me from asking a different but essential question to anyone reading this book. When are we going to face the fact that sexual abuse and molestation are real issues that can't be ignored or *wished* away? The only way this spirit is going to die is when we start talking about it in our homes, with our children, and in our churches.

After the reporter was long gone and my television was off, I wondered if that little girl's mother believed her when she spoke her truth. Or, did it require the video footage for the mother to believe her story?

Those who are victims of sexual abuse do not need closed-circuit television to view their revolving memories. They live with them every day. Dark secrets that are so deep-rooted one wonders if they can ever come out. They are always engaged in spiritual warfare to unshackle themselves from the endless torment.

The reporter said, "the twenty-four-year-old pedophile ran out of his car naked. He was chasing behind the little girl who only had on a t-shirt. He had taken her innocence forever. She will live the rest of her life remembering the moment she cried out, saying, stop, no, please, I want my momma and why! Sadly, she will never have her questions answered. Still, if she trusts in God—he will restore her according to Joel 2:25, "*I will repay you for the years the locusts have eaten—the great locust and the young locust, the other locusts and the locust swarm [a]—my great army that I sent among you.*"

How did he choose her? Did he circle an elementary school for hours looking for a perfect candidate? Did he target the child that he figured would not scream? Did he avoid the one that he suspected would fight back? Or, was she a family friend?"

I have no way of knowing what tactics or selection process the man used, what I am sure of is at some point—either during the act, or afterward, or both—that little girl wondered, *Why me?*

The National Sexual Violence Resource Center (2018) (www. nsvrc.org) reports that people who are victims of sexual abuse are usually targeted by someone they know. Nearly three out of four adolescents (74%) who have been sexually assaulted were victimized by someone they knew *well* (Kilpatrick, Saunders, & Smith, 2003). One-fifth (21.1%) were committed by a family member (Kilpatrick, Saunders, & Smith, 2003).

Why would my dad ever do what he did to me? This question has boggled me for years. To this day, there are times when I fall into the trap of flashbacks. I still cannot fathom why he did it. I could not think through it at six years old, and I am not sure I can completely grasp it now.

Despite the questions that continue to swirl within me, I do know that God is gracious and the forgiver of all sin.

The next time you see a group of children playing in the park, ask yourself this, why is that one girl not jumping rope with everyone else? Why does that little boy have his head tucked to his chest? Why is that girl always yelling, angry, unruly, and continually succeeding at causing trouble? Could she be crying out?

The signs of abuse are not only seen in children. Adults display them as well, think about it. Why is that woman promiscuous? Why do some women have problems making love to her husband? Could any of these actions be a direct result of low self-esteem, or were they sexually abused?

Don't be afraid to ask the questions. If we do not know the signs, we cannot treat the disease. It is not only the first step in solving this age-long dilemma but the beginning of an out-of-the-box generation of thinking.

Problem solvers do not run away from issues. They confront them head-on. Time has come for us to deal with this matter, OUT LOUD. Sexual abuse is real. It affects us. It affects how our country moves forward into the next generation. It affects churches, businesses, families, and society. In 2 Samuel, the Bible tells us the story of Tamar, who was a victim of rape by her stepbrother, but she maintained her character and poise while suffering in silence. There are many Tamar's around us, and we should position ourselves to take notice and provide a space for them to tell their truth.

Jeremiah 29:11 says, *"For I know the plans I have for you. Plans of good and not of evil, give you a hope and a future."* I believe there are people chosen to partake in this sort of betrayal— In my case, it was my father—the man who exposed me to indecency. The man who God chose to raise me. Unfortunately, the devil used him to include me in his sexual fantasies.

Survivors of sexual abuse are like people involved in a head-on collision with an 18-wheeler truck. The truck was meant to kill us, but we refuse to die. We are still here. We are fighting back against the enemy with a vengeance. Yes, there may be times when you feel like running away, crying, and repeatedly asking, "Why Me?" and "Why Us?" but continue to remain steadfast and immovable for the cause of bringing awareness to sexual assault.

Dr. Maya Angelou said, *"We delight in the beauty of the butterfly, but rarely admit the changes it has gone through to achieve that beauty."* I decided to stand. I decided to survive the storm. Yes, I have lost some things along the way. I made stupid mistakes. I had to tread troubled water a few times. There were, and have been, many times when I went under the water, and it felt like I would never come out.

But suddenly, I'd find the strength to lift my hand until it broke the surface of the water. Then my head and body. Once I opened my eyes, I spotted the greatest lifeguard, God. He came through for me. He rescued me. Then God adorned me with His grace. He replaced beauty for ashes, sorrow with love, bitterness with joy, and hurt with hope. God said, *"I can do all things through Christ that strengthens me"* (Philippians 4:13).

God not only knew how I felt but changed the way I think about life. I no longer ask, "Why Me?" Instead, I say, "Why Not Me?"

When God has rescued you, he gives you hope, peace, love, kindness, gentleness, purpose, and clear direction—He is the master surgeon. He is the great Savior for the lost and dying, and a skillful restorer. Do I have hope for this world? Yes, I do. Jesus is the father to the orphan, the husband of the widow, and the comforter of the lost. So, I have no choice but to remain hopeful.

Don't be afraid to ask God to direct you as He did me.

God knows His chosen ones. Sometimes, the problems you must face are more than you wish to cope with, and tomorrow does not seem to offer any solutions. Believe in yourself and your dreams. You will soon realize the future holds great things for you, and the difficult times will not last always.

The End

Readers' Discussion Questions

1. How do you feel about Kassidie?
2. Could you forgive your abuser?
3. Kassidie chose to forgive her father, do you understand why she felt the need to forgive without the "*but*"?
4. What is your take on her allowing her father to have a relationship with her children?
5. What stood out about the book as it relates to being both a victim and a survivor of sexual abuse?

Author's Contact Information

Dr. Ketra L. Davenport-King
Author | Advocate | Consultant

Life After Advocacy Group, Inc.
(940) 227-1615
info@lifeafterag.org
www.lifeafterag.org

Follow on Social Media
Facebook - @AuthorDrKetra
Twitter - @LifeAfterAdvGrp
Instagram - @Author_DrKetra

We Can Help

Life After Advocacy Group

Who Are We?

Life After Advocacy Group, Inc. is a 501c3 non-profit organization committed to promoting awareness and prevention in sexual, verbal, emotional, and physical abuse by identifying, admitting, and advocating education within the church body and local community.

Mission
The mission of LAAG is to assist children, women, and men in promoting a balanced life after being sexually abused by creating a confident, caring, and personal environment.

Vision
Life After Advocacy Group, Inc.'s vision is to be a catalyst for victims of sexual crimes. To rehabilitate the lives of sexually abused and rape victims. To advocate for legislative laws for sexual assault victims and families.

Purpose
To provide support to victims and their family members by educating them on information regarding sexual abuse and neglect.

Signs of a Silent Cry

When children think no one will believe them, or they do not know how to tell us. They will change, and *yes*, it is noticeable:

- Do not want to go to a specific place, or become fearful when around a particular person.
- Show sexual knowledge or behavior beyond their age.
- Overly affectionate and show signs of seductive gestures with peers and adults.
- Recurring genital infections or pain in their genital area.
- Sleeping problems such as bedwetting, nightmares, and fearful of sleeping in a dark room or alone.
- Eating problems.
- Learning disabilities, mental and behavioral problems. The possibility of withdrawing from friends and family.

Communication is Key

Information about sexual abuse can be a part of every child's basic safety knowledge. Begin as early as you think your child will understand.

- Good communication begins with teaching children the correct name of each body part.
- Often, we put off talking about sex with our children because of our discomfort, rather than the child's ability to understand.
- Finding out what your child already knows is the perfect way to begin a conversation.

- Their answer will help you to identify what information they may have received from friends, school, books, T.V., etc. Perfect opportunity to give the correct information

HAVE AN EAR TO HEAR!

The Impact of Sexual Abuse The Life After

It is estimated there are 60 million survivors of childhood sexual abuse in America today.

- Approximately 30% of women in prison stated they had been abused as children.
- Approximately 95% of teenage prostitutes have been sexually abused.
- Long-term effects of child abuse include fear, anxiety, depression, anger, hostility, inappropriate sexual behavior, poor self-esteem, a tendency toward substance abuse, and difficulty with close relationships.
- If the child victim does not resolve the trauma, sexuality may become an area of adult conflict.

When someone tells you, they've been sexually abused

Your reaction has the power to calm or upset a child/adult. **SHOW** your support and willingness to understand.

- Their greatest fear may be that he or she is to **BLAME**.
- **RESPECT** their privacy. Find a private place to **TALK**.
- **RESPOND** to questions and feelings in a calm, matter-of-fact way.
- Give **POSITIVE** messages like: "What the abuser did was wrong" and "I'm sorry that it happened to you" and "I know you are not responsible for what has happened to you."
- **REMEMBER** it can happen as a child, and **AFFECT** you as an adult
- BE **SUPPORTIVE** and **TRUSTING**
- Do not be **JUDGMENTAL!**

Identify | Admit | Accept

When you think you may have been abused as a child... You are not alone

- Nearly 2 million Texans have been sexually assaulted, that is 13% of Texas' population
- 1,479,912 are females and 372,394 are males
- Few victims report their assaults to law enforcement, (20% females, and 12 % males).
- Overall, 18% of victims report assaults to law enforcement.
- Eighty-five percent of victims reported a spouse, partner, date, boyfriend/girlfriend, relative, or acquaintance raped them.

Resources

- Life After Advocacy Group, Inc
  P. O. Box 1412
  Vernon, TX 76385
  (940) 227-1615
  info@lifeafterag.org

- Prevent Child Abuse Texas
  1341 W. Mockingbird Ln, Suite 560W
  Dallas, TX 75247
  (469) 399-6900
  admin@texprotects.org

- Prevent Child Abuse Texas
  512 E. 11th St., Suite 201
  Austin, TX 78701
  (737) 209-8118
  oca@dfps.state.tx.us

- RAINN (Rape, Abuse & Incest National Network)
  www.rainn.org
  (800) 656-HOPE (4673)

- Texas Association Against Sexual Assault
  7700 Chevy Chase Dr., Suite 230
  Austin, Texas 78752
  (512) 474-7190
  infor@taasa.org

References

Information provided by A Health Survey of Texans: A Focus on Sexual Assault (2003) and the National Violence Against Women Study (1996).

Kilpatrick, D. G., Saunders, B. E., & Smith, D. W. (2003). Youth victimization: Prevalence and implications (NIJ Research Brief NCJ 194972). Retrieved from the National Criminal Justice Reference Service: https://www.ncjrs.gov/pdffiles1/nij/194972.pdf

(2020, May 20). Retrieved from National Sexual Violence Resource Center: https://www.nsvrc.org/about-sexual-assault

Bible references

Scriptures noted NIV are taken from the Holy Bible, New International Version*,
NIV* Copyright © 1973, 1978, 1984, 2011 by Biblica, Inc. * Used by permission. All rights reserved worldwide.
Scriptures noted NKJV are taken from the Holy Bible, New King James Version*.
Copyright © 1982 by Thomas Nelson. Used by permission. All rights reserved.
Scriptures noted ESV are taken from The Holy Bible, English Standard Version.
ESV* Text Edition: 2016. Copyright © 2001 by Crossway Bibles, a publishing ministry of Good News Publishers.
Scriptures noted KJV are taken from the Holy Bible, the King James Version, public domain.

Made in the USA
Columbia, SC
29 March 2022

58296968R00061